That
Early Spring

That Early Spring

GUNNEL BECKMAN

Translated from the Swedish by
JOAN TATE

THE VIKING PRESS · NEW YORK

Våren då allting hände (Stockholm, Albert Bonniers Forlag, 1974)
The Loneliness of Mia (London, The Bodley Head, 1975)

First American Edition

Copyright © Gunnel Beckman, 1974
English translation Copyright © The Bodley Head Ltd, 1975
All rights reserved
Published in 1977 by The Viking Press
625 Madison Avenue, New York, N.Y. 10022
Printed in U.S.A.
Library of Congress Cataloging in Publication Data
Beckman, Gunnel.   That early spring.
Translation of Våren då allting hände.
Summary: During one eventful spring, a young Swedish
girl learns about love, independence, and death.
[1. Death—Fiction. 2. Sweden—Fiction] I. Title.
PZ7.B381745Th3 [Fic] 76–13145
ISBN 0–670–69773–7

· *To Susanna* ·

OTHER, if you say that we mustn't forget
to empty the trash cans *again*, I'll scream," said Mia, biting
off the thread. "I promise on my honor that we won't forget
either the trash, or our underwear, or our vitamins, or the
damned hibiscus, or the burners on the stove, or . . ."

"Yes, sorry, darling, but I'm really not in my right mind,"
replied her mother, running a hand over her eyes. "If only
Lillan would come back from those stables. I can't see why
she had to go running off down there at the last minute.
You wait, now we'll miss the train . . ."

Mia's mother was standing by the kitchen table, trying
to cram a pair of child's skates into an already overstuffed
bag, at the same time munching a cheese sandwich and
now and again taking a gulp from a cup on the drainboard.
"Are you nearly done, Mia?"

"Yes, I've just finished."

Mia handed the coat to her mother. "But it isn't very
well sewn."

"That doesn't matter . . . as long as the hem isn't hanging
down. What's the time, now? Look at one that's right . . .
the kitchen clock is always slow. Help, half past eleven
already!"

"But, Mother, there's no hurry. Dad hasn't come yet, and
he's reserved the taxi. Here's Lillan, anyway."

"Oh, thank goodness."

"You've no idea how pleased Alexander and Lady Godiva

were that I went and said good-bye for the last time," cried Lillan, rushing into the kitchen with shining eyes. "Mr. Persson said that he was sure there were tears in Alexander's eyes!"

"Silly . . . hurry up now and get all your things so that you're all ready when Dad comes with the taxi. You haven't forgotten your toothbrush, have you? And your bag of schoolbooks—where's that? And your—"

"There they are down there," called Mia, who had gone over to the window to keep a lookout. "I'll go out and bring up the elevator . . . I'll take the big bag."

"My *Mickey Mouse* . . . I can't find my new *Mickey Mouse* I had for reading on the train!" wailed Lillan, rummaging around the living room. "I *know* I had it in here this morning."

"Come on, now, Lillan. Don't bother about that. Dad'll buy you another at the station. Here, take your wretched skates."

Mia stood on the sidewalk in the bitter wind, watching the taxi driving away. She was shaking with cold, but she stayed until the taxi was out of sight, until she could no longer see Mother's and Lillan's eager waving hands through the back window. Her mouth and cheeks were wet from their last rough kisses.

"We'll write often, Mia. Look after yourself . . . Oh, Mia, try to understand."

A few hasty kisses, a big hug, a taxi door slamming— and a period of your life disappears around the corner, almost the whole of your childlhood.

Write often. Try to understand.

As Mia went up in the elevator, she began to weep. Her heart was aching in a way she had never felt before, aching explosively like a bad tooth. Thank goodness she had managed to keep back the tears until now. Ever since this morning she and her mother had hardly dared to look at each other. They had both known that if either of them had weakened for one moment, they would have rushed into each other's arms and wept. And they simply hadn't had time for that.

But now she had all the time in the world.

Mia went around the empty apartment, silently and still, without sobbing, now and again wiping her face with the sleeve of her sweater or snatching a paper towel from the roll in the kitchen.

The apartment was like a battlefield, the dishes from breakfast still on the table, records pulled out all around the record player, newspapers on the floor, bedclothes on the terrace, and abandoned toys on the hall floor. In the bathroom she found the *Mickey Mouse* comic and a pair of dirty pants.

Mia walked around without touching anything, just feeling the ache and seeing all the emptiness. Clothes taken from their hangers, bottles and brushes and cream jars gone from the bathroom, Lillan's black riding hat . . . the photograph of Mia that used to hang above Mother's bed. All that remained were the smells, the horrible stinking memories—Mother's eau de cologne, Lillan's models and old riding shirt, cigarette butts in the ashtrays.

And right through everything, the persistent spicy smell of the three batches of ginger cookies burned one after another on that awful afternoon a few days before Christmas when Grandpa had suddenly telephoned to say that he had found Mother a job in an office, a job that had to be taken up immediately after Twelfth-night! Before that, they had been saying that Mother and Lillan would not be going down to Åsa until about January 15. Then suddenly there was hardly any time.

It was ridiculous that ten days should make such a big difference when they were going to be separated for a whole school term later on. But it was as if none of them had really been able to face the thought of parting before— they had all consciously or unconsciously tucked away the whole departure until after the Christmas holidays. There was such a *long* time until January 15—almost a month— time enough. First this damned . . . no, no . . . this happy Christmas had to be celebrated.

Anyway, they had all had such an awful lot to do during the week before Christmas that there hadn't really been time to worry about what was going to happen afterward, especially Mother, who had had to work overtime for her firm, and Mia, who had been working herself to death at the florist's. Not to mention Lillan, who was to be a hobgoblin in her school Christmas play and needed help with making the ears and tail. Well, for heaven's sake, it was enough to drive anyone crazy.

Then that telephone call from Grandpa came along and upset every one of them.

Dad got a terrible migraine and had to refuse the invitation to an official Christmas dinner, and Mother had a nosebleed and burned one batch of ginger cookies after another. Even Lillan, who had up to then been living in a kind of unreal rush of excitement at the thought of Grandpa's horses and Granny's kittens, was afflicted with sudden insight and cried herself to sleep. And Mia herself almost threw an azalea plant worth forty kronor at a silly customer.

That you survived at all was extraordinary enough.

Mia put on the record Jan had given her for Christmas and let Björn Skifs scrape away at "Never My Love" and "Muddy Waters," but that didn't make things any better.

Perhaps she ought to try to straighten up a bit . . . but Dad wasn't coming home until dinner time.

Mia went into the living room and stood by the window.

The big yard with its deserted play equipment and bare barberry bushes lay shabby with dirty snow. A child in yellow rubber boots was splashing water in the middle of a large puddle. Between the high apartment buildings in the shopping center, she could just see the communal Christmas tree, disheveled and wind blown in the gusty January wind. The smoke from the district heating center was floating like a sooty snake around the clocktower of the concrete church over toward the high school's tiled roof and the empty framework of the stadium grandstand. If you hadn't been miserable before, then you soon would be, looking out on this wretched winter day.

Couldn't they at least take away that damned Christmas tree soon . . .

Of course, yes. Mia turned back into the room. That was true. It was almost the last thing Mother had said. "Don't forget to take the decorations off the tree and ask Dad to help you out with it before Elsa Eriksson comes to clean tomorrow."

Mia went over to the tree. It smelled green and good and was only just beginning to lose its pine needles. Any other year it would have been heartrending to throw out a Christmas tree that looked so alive and fresh. But not now. Now it would be a pleasure to pull the decorations off it and heave it out into the yard or wherever it had to be heaved. Like taking some kind of revenge; revenge against this Christmas that since just before Advent had been one long nightmare.

With determined steps Mia went out to the kitchen cupboard to find the basket in which they kept the Christmas decorations, which would now lie there getting even more crumpled and faded, waiting for another Christmas.

Another Christmas. What would that be like—it was good not to know.

It couldn't be worse than this one, anyway.

She put the last red glass ball back into the basket. Now there was nothing left but the silver star on the top and a little crumpled bird. Mia carefully freed the black thread from the sticky branch and stood still with the bird in her hand. It was one she had made with Miss Jonsson in the first grade . . . at her old elementary school by the sea.

With the bird in her hand, she went over and sat down in the corner of the sofa, a great tiredness coming over her. She pulled her legs up under her and sat staring out into the gray mist of the winter light. It was only two o'clock.

Mia loved this strange peaceful hour when darkness slowly fell. She had read somewhere in a book about someone who also loved the dusk—*the very word is angora soft and comforting . . . sounds change . . . contours soften . . . the earth slows down . . . one swings in a hammock between light and darkness . . .*

But this cold grayness was no comfort.

Suddenly it seemed to her that she was the most un-happy person in the whole world, so unhappy that it was no use crying any longer; she simply allowed herself to be filled with a sense of loneliness so hopeless and heavy that it was as if someone had flung a suffocating cloth over her head. As if . . . as if there were no longer any air left in the room, as if the very silence in the empty apartment were evil and threatening. As if nothing would ever be fun again.

Strange, she thought vaguely, crushing the bird in her hand so that it became even more crumpled. It's strange, but this is almost worse than before Christmas, when I thought I was pregnant.

Then she had been absolutely certain that nothing in the whole world could be worse than the paralyzing waiting for her period—that confusion of hope and fear and doubt, and that horrible responsibility that you didn't know what to do with.

At the time, she had thought that as long as this was cleared up, then everything would be all right, and of course it was marvelous that things turned out as they did. She had been lucky not to have to pay for her own stupidity . . . or thoughtlessness or inexperience, whatever you called it.

Though she had probably paid a price.

She thought about that first awful evening after her period had come, when she laid there in bed with the elec-tric blanket and a tea tray, just waiting to feel relieved and exhilarated. And instead she was possessed by a throbbing black anxiety . . . anxiety because she did not recognize her-self and did not understand her own reactions; disappointment over Jan just sounding cheerful over the telephone, now that everything was over . . . now everything would be as before.

It was that horrible evening, too, when Mother came in to talk about the divorce and Mia felt she didn't have the energy to face it, ashamed that she appeared indifferent and strange in the eyes of her poor unknowing mother.

But Dad helped her, sat by her bed and held her hand, explaining that it was shock, the backlash after all that tension; that it was quite natural and others felt like that, too. Strange, that everything became so much easier to bear when you knew you weren't alone.

But at the moment, everything seemed in some way even more wretched.

And now there was no one around to comfort her.

Dad was the last person she could go to now. He would probably come home from work just as depressed as she was, full of anxiety about what was going to happen . . . missing Lillan . . . worrying over whether Mia and he would get along together. She couldn't just throw herself into his arms and cry because she was so lonely, because she was missing her mother. A painful, childish longing for Mommy.

And Gran—she couldn't do that either.

It would be like complaining that Mother and Dad had simply been cruel and arranged a divorce! When they had talked about it, Gran and Mia, one day before Christmas, Mia had tried to appear oh so brave and had said that it was all for the best and it would surely work out. They hadn't met since then. Gran had had a cold and hadn't come for Christmas, and since then visitors had been banned from the old people's home because of the risk of influenza.

And Jan?

The whole family thought she had Jan.

"When's Jan coming back from Norrland?" Mother had asked anxiously the evening before. "It's nice that you've got Jan, my darling."

Nice that you've got Jan. Well, had she? Had he got her?

That was what was difficult. She no longer knew how things stood with Jan. She thought now that she no longer knew a single thing about Jan, that she had really never known anything at all, that she didn't even know what she herself felt. They had in some way drifted apart since that business of the child that never was a child. It was as if the fear had destroyed their pleasant everyday relationship and opened . . . well, like opening a window out toward . . . the future.

Perhaps things would have been better if they had spent a little time trying to understand each other. But it wasn't all that easy to understand other people when one didn't even understand oneself.

Just trying to understand what they called being in love.

What was it, in fact? And how did one fall in love? It seemed such a matter of chance. Was it just that when a more or less acceptable guy got it into his head to fall for you, then you took it for granted you'd fall in love with him? You'd be pleased that someone had chosen you! Flattered, quite simply. So you'd fall in love with him, bong! Especially if he danced well and had kind brown eyes.

But they had had fun together, got on well together—hadn't they?—talked, gone for walks, had a beer, gone to the movies, even slept with each other—was that enough?

She didn't know. All she knew was that the only time

she had seen Jan before he went to stay with his uncle in Norrland before Christmas, everything had gone wrong.

Mia had thought and thought about that evening hundreds of times, trying to understand both Jan and herself.

If only they had been able to meet at once after her period had come and Jan had returned from a game in Eskilstuna. But then Jan went and caught the flu and was in bed at his parents' house. They weren't even able to talk to each other on the phone. And then his job in Norrland came along and all in such a hurry; a temporary job with some uncle in Matfors or wherever it was.

Of course, he had to take it; he was unemployed. But at that moment and in such a rush? Just when they needed to meet often and talk . . . and sort of build, yes, build up something new. If there was anything to talk about. It didn't seem as if Jan thought there was all that much to talk about. He just thought that they would have a nice evening on the old pattern—have a meal, drink a little wine, sit in front of the fire, munch vanilla wafers, and so on . . . as before.

"Mia, darling . . . I suppose you've got hold of . . . well, something safe . . . the pill, or something?"

It was almost the first thing he had said when they got inside the door with their bags of food.

"I certainly have not!"

"What—why not? I thought it was obvious . . . then we can't!"

"For God's sake, what *do* you mean? You know as well as I do that I can't take the pill because I'm so irregular, and there are long lines at those clinics where you get coils and so on."

"But there are private doctors, aren't there?"

"Yes, but *I* can't afford that! Anyway, I must say I've actually had other things to think about this last week besides contraceptives! First, I had a hellishly long and troublesome period, so that I nearly died, and then we've had endless tests at school, and Mother and Dad are separating, and . . . and then you come along and carry on about contraceptives! It seems as if you never think about anything else except going to bed . . . just as if that was the most important thing in the world."

"But, Mia . . . Mia darling . . . don't be so angry. I'm sorry, for God's sake—I didn't think . . . I was anxious to keep us from getting into the same damned mess again."

"You weren't all that worried we'd get into a mess last autumn," she snapped. "Then it was oh so safe with condoms, wasn't it, and then I was the one who was worried and stupid, wasn't I?"

"But, Mia, don't you see . . . that I got a shock, too. Thinking it over, it would have been damned awkward."

"And you who were so eager for me to leave school and stay in the kitchen and cook your meals."

"I wasn't. But, of course, I had to stand by you."

"The virtuous guy who stands by you and offers protection and a wedding ring."

"What the hell's the matter with you? Why do you sounds to damned—"

"Perhaps you've *forgotten* I had no intention of marrying you. Perhaps you've forgotten I was thinking of getting an abortion, if it'd been anything—perhaps you happen to have forgotten that?"

"Oh, I didn't believe that—"

"You didn't believe it? Didn't you *believe* I'd have the courage, is that it? Did you really think I was just going to go around letting myself be protected—that I didn't have a mind of my own?"

"But, Mia, I don't understand a damned thing. You go and have a hell of a time thinking you're pregnant—me too . . . and when I ask you if you've got hold of something safer, so that we don't have to go through all that again—then you get furious and shout at me! And not only that, but also because I suggested before that we should get married, if you really were pregnant. I couldn't very well know what you thought about abortion, could I? There's no darned sense in what you say. I don't understand a blasted thing."

"No, because of course you can't understand a simple thing like me imagining that our . . . our relationship was something more than just eating a bit and drinking a bit and then rushing into bed! That I was stupid enough to think that after all we've been through, which just might have brought us a little closer to each other . . . well, that we in fact would have lots to say to each other about how things are for us . . . and how it . . . in some way has changed us and that . . ."

And then she had burst into tears.

Kindly, Jan tried to comfort her and explain. He hadn't understood how she felt, she was tired and depressed about her parents' divorce, he'd been awfully stupid, now they'd have a meal and light the fire and blow their noses.

So Mia of course pulled herself together and washed her face at the sink and began to peel potatoes, while Jan got logs and set the table, now and again patting her a little fumblingly on the back.

They politely chewed away at their pork chops and drank a glass of Algerian wine each and looked at the fire and talked about Christmas and about Jan's uncle's factory in Matfors and listened politely to Olrog and "Journey to Cythera." And the vanilla wafers tasted like sawdust in their mouths and it was altogether a perfectly dreadful evening.

Finally they kissed for a while in the entrance of Mia's apartment building and said Merry Christmas, then, and have a good time, and don't overdo it, and we'll write, and I'll probably be back in the middle of January . . . well, Merry Christmas again . . . and . . . bye, then.

After that, there was an exchange of Christmas records and a somewhat unsuccessful telephone call from Matfors, full of how are you and thanks for the record, it was great, there's lots of snow here, it's foggy here and slushy, and what's the job like and you'll tell me all about it when you come back, won't you, and good luck to you. And bye, then . . .

Mia began to walk back and forth across the floor, kicking at a pile of old comics that Lillan had pulled out in her hunt for *Mickey Mouse*. She took a bite out of a half-eaten marzipan pig that had been lying on the table.

Help, what the place looked like! Under the desk was Lillan's recorder, which they'd hunted like mad for this morning . . . together with a torn-off hobgoblin's ear.

If only she could get some kind of sensible letter off to Jan. But what could she say when she had no idea what needed saying? Oh, God, if only she at least had someone to talk to about all this. It was idiotic that she never had a chance to tell the whole story to Mother before she left. But it just didn't come about. She simply couldn't burden her mother with that as well.

Anyway, things had been somewhat strained between Mia and her mother since before Christmas, as if Mother thought Mia were taking sides with Dad in some way.

And she wasn't.

At first, when Dad told her about it that evening, she felt a strange rage against them both, because they had betrayed her; because they weren't happy; because they'd been unhappy for a long time. Her whole childhood suddenly seemed a great betrayal, a pretending game that she hadn't seen through, a security that was empty inside.

She shouted at Dad, as if the whole divorce were an insult to her and Lillan.

And Dad wept.

And suddenly the rage melted away and she began to understand a little.

"Try to understand," Mother had whispered.

And yet it was only her own loneliness, her own heartache, that Mia was concerned with.

She turned on the radio.

Request program from Jockmock . . . a southern woman who loved mountains . . . another female who wanted to hear, "Listen you there, come with me, you're the girl I want to see." On another station a dignified snotty guy was announcing that they were just about to hear the tragic finale in the fifth act, in which Manon dies in her lover's arms.

Finnish language course . . . oh, hopeless.

Supposing she were to phone Barbro?

She hadn't actually seen Barbro since that crummy birthday party at the end of November, that awful evening when Mia had tried to cause a miscarriage by racing seven floors up the emergency stairs!

They hadn't actually met many times since last spring, when they both left their old school and went on to different ones. Because they both had boyfriends. At her new school, Mia hadn't had time to become special friends with anyone, except perhaps Lena, who sat next to her. She was very nice. But when people know you have a boyfriend whom they don't know, you get left out. They think you don't want to go to parties, or to the movies, or to a discotheque, and that kind of thing. And you don't, mostly, so then you get left out like that.

But Stefan—Barbro's boyfriend—was perhaps away for the holidays. He came from Örebro, or somewhere like that.

It would be marvelous to see Barbro again and have a real chat, like in the old days when they'd been neighbors and in the same class and best friends and shared everything from Beatles records to math homework and confidences. Heavens, what a lot of marvelous talk had risen from Barbro's rickety old patched leather armchairs over secret cigarettes and popcorn.

But then Barbro chose the social-studies track, and she decided on the technical track, so they parted, although it was true to say that they had drifted apart quite a lot during their last year at school. Barbro was always more forward than Mia when it came to boys, and Mia was probably a little envious. And Barbro didn't like it that Mia became a bookworm.

The last few times, in fact, they didn't have all that much to talk about, and for the first time in years, they didn't give each other a small Christmas present. They just met hurriedly in the shopping center and said Merry Christmas and heavens, how hectic everything was, and we must meet again sometime.

What was her number again? Don't tell me you can't even remember that!

"Hello, Aunt Elsa, this is Mia Järeberg. Is Barbro at home by any chance? Oh, is she? She's been in Örebro all over Christmas? Oh, I see . . . but she'll be back soon won't she, because school starts again on Monday. What—she's left school? But what a surprise . . . why? She's going to get *married*? Oh, good gracious, and I never knew a thing about it! Oh, it's only just been decided. Oh . . . I see . . . oh, *is* she? Is that why!"

It turned out to be a long conversation with Barbro's mother.

Afterward, Mia remained sitting on the telephone stool in the hall, quite dizzy from everything she'd heard.

It was crazy.

It was all absolutely crazy.

Barbro was expecting a child in May and was getting married at the end of this month. Glory be. In a white veil and all.

Then she must have been already three months pregnant at her birthday party! It was crazy. Yes, someone had even pulled her leg about her at last getting a bosom of some kind in her old age.

But no one was told anything until the week before Christmas.

In itself it wasn't all that strange that Barbro hadn't been able to bring herself to talk to her mother, who had had an awful time with Agneta's little baby boy all that autumn. But she could have· talked to Agneta, who was a nurse. Well, that was easy to say—listen to Mia, who had fussed around, not even going to the drugstore.

Anyway, perhaps Barbro had *wanted* to have a child. She seemed to be head over heels in love with Stefan; she admired him enormously and was very proud he had chosen her—and he such a magnet to girls, too.

"They've rented an apartment in Örebro. Stefan's going to start working for his father . . . and they want a church wedding, the silly young idiots."

Aunt Elsa almost spat out the words. "So now she's probably knitting sacques and making maternity dresses, too! Though that's good, as long as she thinks she's in love with Stefan and he with her. She's playing dollhouses like a five-year-old . . . as long as it lasts.

"Yes, I suppose you think it sounds terrible, Mia," she went on, "but I'm so *tired*. Tired of children yelling, tired of being a woman, and tired of irresponsible kids leaping into bed and getting pregnant and having children they can't cope with. To tell you the truth, I almost begin to long for the good old days when it was "in" to be moral. No, no, Mia, dear, I know, I *know*, you needn't protest, but all the same, it's time people saw that all this sexual freedom entails *responsibility*. Instead, you can't even open a magazine without reading about sixteen-year-olds complaining about not getting the right sort of orgasm! And I read somewhere else that abortions for thirteen-year-olds had trebled in the last year. That's really mad! Yes, I've nothing against free abortion, but what's needed now is quite different information from what young people get today, although one thought that was all well arranged nowadays.

"It's we parents, of course, who don't see to it properly, or soon enough," Barbro's mother went on. "But one doesn't like waking sleeping dogs, so to speak. And now it's become so that Barbro doesn't *dare* talk to me, although I've been on at her not to give in until she'd got the pill or whatever. I even offered to go with her to the doctor . . . but, oh, no . . . she didn't want that. 'Things aren't what you think, Mom,' she said. And then you don't like to go on and on, 'cause you know it's a tricky subject—and then look what happens! You don't know whether to laugh or cry.

"And you don't really know what to do about it, either. There should be easily accessible advice bureaus where boys and girls could go and get sensible advice. Not just on contraceptives—though that's important enough—but something on responsibility and, how shall I put it, morals, morality, and sex . . . and what's going to happen to all those unwanted little children?

"And I really do think that it's time girls pulled themselves together a little and didn't let themselves be blackmailed into bed, just because the boy threatens to go elsewhere. Yes, I'm sorry, Mia dear, to be going on so like this, but I've been alone here at home all over Christmas, looking after little Jonas—Agneta is working at the hospital now and is hardly ever free—and so I've got myself worked up into such a state, I'm almost bursting. How will there ever be any equality, when so many girls risk never getting a proper training . . . but go and get landed with a kid and then perhaps the father leaves them, and they have to be content with badly paid jobs and Social Security benefits. If their mothers don't help, of course, but that won't go on much longer. I wouldn't have given my job up to look after Jonas if he hadn't been ill, and if Agneta hadn't had so little left to do of her nurse's training."

Actually, it had been nice listening to Aunt Elsa's outburst. Mia wished only that she had had the courage to tell her that if there were anyone in the world who understood it all, then it was Mia. But it hadn't been worth dragging all that up, now that it was all over.

But it *was* nice to listen to Aunt Elsa, to listen to another woman, a grown woman talking like that, like some kind of support. And poor Barbro—it must be awfully hard work going round being the happy bride-to-be if her mother went on like that.

Mia began walking around the apartment again. She really would have to straighten it up a bit now. It was already past four and she must at least clean up the worst of it and put the potatoes on before Dad came home.

Her thoughts continued to whirl around Barbro.

Strange, contradictory feelings rose inside her and gnawed at her.

First a tremendous relief that she wasn't in Barbro's shoes, though it was a pretty awful feeling at the same time a kind of triumph—"that-didn't-happen-to-me-anyway"— when she had been so close to being in the same situation herself.

And then a horrid little feeling of *envy*. That eternal old dollhouse instinct—get-married-and-have-children–longing, which she had in fact also felt in the middle of all that awful waiting. But then something else, too—a nudge forward, a confirmation that what she herself had decided was right; that it was important not to weaken again.

Suddenly Mia felt in a much better mood. The numbing sense of loneliness had lifted a little, her tears now under control, and she even began singing as she rinsed out cups and swept up crumbs. Outside the window the comforting dusk fell . . . a hammock between darkness and light . . .

Now she could ring up Gran without risking bursting into tears, and when she heard Gran's voice on the telephone, she was filled with a tenderness which suddenly seemed like security. The voice contained a note of self-assurance that was infectious.

Gran wanted to know whether Mother and Lillan had got off all right, of course.

"Well, I wouldn't say all right, exactly," said Mia, "but they got off."

"Poor Marianne," said Gran. "Things are going to be difficult for her."

"They're going to be difficult for all of us . . ."

"Yes, of course . . . but you see . . . breaking away from your own home like that—when you've been married for so long—and going back to your mother and father, that isn't easy. And then being separated from you—from an adult daughter. It's not the same with a child like Lillan . . . of course, she's a good distraction when one's miserable, but there's a difference with an adult daughter you can talk to, you see."

"But Dad needs me, too . . ."

"Yes, yes, but you're both still at home. Think of your mother starting a strange new job, too, a job she has to be especially successful in, just because her father got it for her. But she's strong and hard-working, Marianne is, and she'll manage, I expect. You'll write to her often, won't you? She'll want to hear all the little details."

"All right, I'll try," said Mia, "though letterwriting's not exactly my strong point."

No, it certainly wasn't easy.

Darling Mother had sat there for over half an hour, at the top of a blank sheet of paper, while Mia sat staring out of the window. The melted snow was streaming down the windowpane and the neighbor's radio was tuned into a request program for people who were ill. There had just been something about the golden halls of heaven.

Mia thought about what Gran had said, and she thought about her mother's voice on the telephone the evening before, when she'd called from Åsa to tell them they had arrived safely. Mother sounded so terribly tired and depressed, although you could hear that she was trying to pull herself together. She asked lots of unnecessary questions, as if she had forgotten that she had only left home that same day; as if lots of things could have happened in those few hours.

"I *have* emptied the trash cans, Mother, and taken lots and lots of vitamins, and watered the hibiscus," joked Mia.

"Are you all right, you two?" Mother asked.

What could you answer to that? Whatever you said, she would be miserable.

"Were the rissoles good?"

"Yes, very good . . . we ate them all."

"But what'll you have for dinner tomorrow?"

"Mother, darling, don't worry so. We'll have some *food* all right."

Afterward Mia and Dad had sat in front of the television, saying nothing, just staring at moronic young men telling smutty stories, neither daring to turn it off.

Then the telephone rang again, and Dad went out to answer it. Although he closed the door behind him and spoke in a low voice, Mia heard what he was saying all the same. It was clearly someone wanting him to do something for him.

"No, however much I'd like to do it, I simply can't take it on. You know, my elder daughter and I are ... on our own this term, and I have to ... no, I can't ... no, I just can't manage it."

"To jump from one thing to another—when's Jan coming home?" asked Dad after he came back. Just as Mother did the evening before.

"I don't know, actually ... he was going to write when he knew."

And then Dad patted her hand kindly and said, "Well, old girl, don't worry about being abandoned. I won't break my word."

"I know, Dad."

Won't break my word. God, how hopeless. How blasted awful everything was.

Dad gave her two sleeping tablets and poured himself a large whisky.

Darling Mother,
Hope you're well.

Heavens, how ridiculous it sounded. WELL. I am well, how are you . . .

Good that the trip went well, even if you did forget Lillan's skates on the train, but they'll turn up again. We're fine here. Elsa Eriksson has just been here and cleaned up. It was needed. I took the ornaments off the Christmas tree and Dad threw it down from the balcony. Elsa sends her love. Her mother-in-law has died and they're going to Borlänge for the funeral, so we'll have to clean up ourselves next week.

It's thawing today and horrible weather, even worse than yesterday. We're having fish sticks for dinner with spinach and gooseberry fool.

I had a card from Jan today—he's staying to work in Matfors for the time being. It's good that he's earning money, even if his uncle doesn't pay all that much. In case you were wondering, I'm not especially sad. It was probably coming to an end, anyway.

It was true, actually. Not just something she'd wanted to write to comfort her mother.

Mia looked at the last sentence again; it was as if it had written itself. Suddenly the thought had crystallized and steered her pen. "I'm not especially sad. It was probably coming to an end, anyway."

Another piece of news—Barbro is getting married in a few weeks' time. She's expecting a baby in May! I spoke to Aunt Elsa for at least half an hour on the telephone yesterday afternoon. She was tired and very annoyed. A church wedding! I promise to watch out if another guy turns up! I promise on my honor—the trash, vitamins, underwear, the burners, the plants, and—contraceptives.

Oh, Mother, how silly it seems writing letters. But I'll learn, I suppose. I miss you very much—both of you. I thought it'd be nice to give my ears a rest from Lillan for a while—but it isn't true. It's as silent as a tomb here.

That evening Dad and Mia went to see an old James Bond film at the Cosmorama in the center of town. Afterward they went to Svensson's Corner and had open shrimp sandwiches in dim lighting. Jan's friends said hello to Mia and asked where he was. In the square they met the chairman of the local council and his wife. Mia saw them turning around and whispering.

"Tomorrow we're invited out to dinner with Aunt Vera," said Dad as they went up in the elevator.

"Do we *have* to go? It's always so noisy and messy with all those kids," sighed Mia.

"Yes, we must, really. They've asked us out of sheer kindness."

"Exactly."

$\mathcal{M}$IA woke up in the night and had an idea.

She didn't know how it had come, whether it was a dream or something else down in her subconscious which had just popped up. It was simply there, just as she turned over in bed and looked at the clock to see that it was half past two.

Suddenly Mia was so wide awake that she could hardly lie still.

Wouldn't it be a marvelous idea—if Gran came and lived with her and Dad this term? For a while at least, to see if she liked it!

Mia had lain thinking about loneliness for a long time before she had fallen asleep, her thoughts whirling and finally coming to rest on her grandmother, Gran, her father's mother.

She remembered the day when she had gone to see Gran on her name day, Astrid; the time of her unsuccessful pregnancy test. When Gran said . . . almost to herself, "And yet the only thing we really long for is someone who'd have time to talk sensibly to us . . . to know we mean something to an individual person. That it really matters we are actually *alive*."

Strange she remembered that . . . almost word for word, when at the time Mia had had so many troubles of her own overshadowing everything else. She protested quite anxiously and asked whether Gran didn't like the Home, and then Gran said, "For goodness' sake, don't think I want to come and live with you at home . . . I couldn't cope with that. You see, it's just that sometimes I don't like this exhausting life."

But then she dropped the subject and went on about Christmas-present lists.

She said then that she couldn't cope with living with them all, but she must have had Lillan in mind. There must be a terrific difference between living with a family of four, with a young child like Lillan, who was noisy and talkative and brought back lots of friends, than with two quiet people like Dad and Mia.

There must be *all the difference in the world*!

Of course, Mia and Dad got on well together and had

come much closer to each other than before, since that harassing time before Christmas. But at the same time, she already realized how difficult it was going to be if the two of them were to go around being so damned sacrificial and considerate toward each other all the time.

That would be unbearable.

But just think if Gran could come and live with them— then all that would be taken care of. She would be there all the time, like a nice warm stove, that you could warm yourself against when you came home cold and tired and hungry and longing for someone to talk to at the kitchen table. Someone who was there and who could bother to listen and who didn't have regional plans and budgets on her mind all the time.

But the best thing would be that Gran would have some-one to talk to as well. Someone of her own. Dad would be bound to think it fine to be able to do something for Gran —he'd said so many times it was on his conscience that he didn't have time to go and see her often enough. Mother always said the same—Gran is my guilty conscience.

It sounded so awful.

"You needn't get up this early, Mia, love," her father said next morning when she came into the kitchen just before nine. "It's Saturday today."

"Yes, but there's something I simply must talk to you about," said Mia eagerly. "Something I thought of in the night. Dad, couldn't we ask Gran to come and live with us here for this term? Then she'd have company and we . . . I mean . . . I know she longs for someone to talk to."

"Has Gran complained about not liking the Home?" asked Dad, frowning.

"No, not in that way . . . of course she likes it. It's so comfortable and grand, everything there. But I had a feeling last fall that all the same she thinks the life there is rather . . . dull or something. She doesn't enjoy knitting cardigans and gossiping about the Reverend Hammerberg and that kind of thing. Couldn't she come here, Dad, *couldn't she?*"

Mia flung her arms round her father's neck from behind and pressed her cheek against his, so she didn't see the expression on his face, which was far from enthusiastic.

"We—ell," he said slowly. "That's something only Mom can decide, if she really wants to. It wouldn't surprise me if she prefers the quiet and orderliness and the daily routine of the Home."

"But it's quiet here now, now there's only you and me."

"But, Mia dear, she needs care and nursing."

"She can cope with dressing herself and eating. . . . She's only a bit stiff, so that she can't sew or lift heavy things."

"Then there's another matter," said Dad. "I'm not sure, from the purely official point of view, whether you can do that, when someone's been allocated a place in an old people's home. You probably lose it then and have to go on a waiting list all over again, and just think if Mom didn't like it here or, worse still, if she fell ill, and with nowhere to go. It would be irresponsible—"

"But, Dad, surely it doesn't have to be so *complicated*. We could try it out first, and if you pay for her at the Home, then they must let her go back surely? Dad . . . listen, Dad . . . it'd be awful if people weren't able to go away for a while if they wanted to, just because of all those silly formalities."

"You know her heart isn't all that strong."

"A doctor could come here just as easily as to the Home —there isn't a doctor available there all the time, either, and I could leave my door open at night so that I'd hear if she called."

"But, Mia dear, you've got school—"

"Oh, Dad, and I thought you'd think it was such a good idea," said Mia, her voice thickening as she went and stood over by the window.

"Mia, Gran is so well fixed up over there. She's told me so many times, and things are good for the two of us here in peace and quiet. I don't think you can imagine how troublesome it can be, looking after a sick old person."

"You talk as if she were absolutely helpless. And she's not! And I'm not afraid of the trouble. . . . I think it'd be marvelous to . . . anyway, perhaps we could get one of those visiting homemakers that Barbro's grandmother has . . . who comes for a few hours in the daytime. You who're buddies with the council people and suchlike, couldn't you arrange that, Dad? Wouldn't it be fun to be able to do something for Gran for once, and not just let her sit there like a little fish in an aquarium, waiting to die?"

"How you do exaggerate . . ."

"Don't you remember that lecture you gave last year to the Pensioners' Society. You talked about how important it was to give old people an active and meaningful old age. *Have you forgotten that?*"

Mia's father sat silently rubbing his glasses. It was clear that he was struggling with himself.

"Uhuh," he said finally. "Don't think I don't appreciate that you want to do something for Gran. But the most important thing undoubtedly is her own well-being. First I must investigate the formalities of that kind of temporary move, and I'll talk to her doctor as well. If he advises against it, then the matter is closed. Not until that's done, I think, can we ask Gran herself. It'd be unfair to hold out prospects of something that can't happen."

"So you think she'd like to come then?" exclaimed Mia triumphantly. "Oh, thanks, darling Dad . . . That's really good of you. I can ask the superintendent today on the telephone, can't I?"

"I'll see to this," said Dad firmly. "The superintendent doesn't decide things like this. We'll have to wait anyway until the ban on visiting is lifted."

"Oh, Dad, how *glad* I am," cried Mia, dancing around the kitchen so that her hair flopped around her face and one slipper flew under the refrigerator.

"Silly," said Dad, with the first smile of the conversation, and he went over and kissed her on the cheek. "You're a sweet girl."

But Mia had danced her dance of joy a little prematurely.

Her bright idea met with resistance in a quarter she had not even considered—from her mother. Dad insisted that the first thing they had to do was to call and ask Mother.

"That's the most stupid and irresponsible idea I've ever heard," she cried. "Dragging away poor old Gran, who's so well looked after and likes it there at the Home, to an apartment that's only cleaned once a week and meals are any old way . . . and who will give her a bath and help her with all the thousand little things she has to do, and electric blankets and medicine bottles?"

"*I'm* going to do that . . . and then perhaps we can get a visting homemaker sometimes."

"Don't imagine you'll get a homemaker when you've taken someone who's already got a place away to a family where there are adult healthy people! How *can* Dad have agreed to anything so crazy? Mia, dear, you must see . . . how can you think that Gran would like it, sitting alone and deserted all day, while you and Dad are out?"

"I'm sure she'd like it."

"Has she said so?"

"No, not exactly . . ."

"But, Mia dear, don't you see . . . just think, when you want to put a record on . . ."

But then Mia flung down the receiver and ran weeping into her room, throwing herself down on the bed. Dad had to come and take over the call, which became a long and heated one.

Mia never found out what made her mother give way in the end.

Neither did either of them ever find out what Gran said to the doctor when he went to ask her what she herself thought of the suggestion.

"I'm not really terribly enthusiastic about letting you out on this venture, Mrs. Järeberg," the doctor said. "Your heart is unreliable, and as far as I can see, there wouldn't be the same calm and regular attention as at the Home. I'd really advise against it."

"Then this is what I've got to say, doctor. Nothing on earth would stop me going there, now that they want me. You must see, doctor, how fantastic it is for an old person like me, who's already been discarded, so to speak, who sits here day in and day out and just *survives* instead of living—to think that someone really needs her still . . . to think that a young girl like Mia is prepared to cope with a lot of trouble and sacrifices to have me around. Can't you see, doctor, that it's worth the risk of shortening one's miserable life a bit? I'm not that pitiable."

Gran's cheeks had turned quite red with fervor.

The doctor laughed. "Well, then there's nothing for me to do but wash my hands of you, Mrs. Järeberg, and wish you luck. If anything's wrong, just call me and I'll come . . ."

And so it came about that within less than a week, Gran was installed in Lillan's old room, which had been thoroughly cleaned and refurnished, of course. Gran's large comfortable armchair and a number of other things had been brought from the Home, and when Saturday arrived, there she sat in her becoming corduroy housecoat and her silver-white little-girl bangs, with tulips on the table and Grandad on the bookcase.

"Oh, how pleased I am you're here!" said Mia, flitting about the room, arranging and fiddling, moving bottles and jars, putting the eau de cologne within reach, trying to find the right place for Gran's radio, and asking at least eighteen times if she wanted the rug round her knees or a cushion behind her back.

"Mia dear, the idea isn't to kill off poor Gran the very first day," said Dad, frowning.

But Gran just smiled and surreptitiously wiped a few drops of sweat from her forehead.

It wasn't just Gran's moving in that made Mia so happy and expectant. It had also been surprising fun to go back to school.

Suddenly it seemed as if her class belonged and wasn't just a whole lot of individuals who had been gathered up from different schools, full of the loss of old friends, familiar buildings, established nicknames and also full of prejudices when confronted with new and unknown things. Mia felt this especially strongly because she had been almost completely caught up in her own and Jan's world all fall.

But now it seemed actually quite nice and cozy to tumble into their large dirty-yellow classroom, and have her back thumped by Leffe and Lennart, and hear Lena cry, "What a fantastic jacket—did you get it for Christmas?" and "We'll sit next to each other like last term, shall we?" And the principal's bald head glinted like the sun through the corridors and their new Swedish teacher was a smart girl in jeans and gold-rimmed glasses . . .

And behind Mia's back, she heard Svante and Benka whispering, "Have you seen Järeberg? She's become a real knockout."

After school she and Lena went to the Paris Café and had chocolate goodies, and each confided her situation to the other.

That is, Mia told Lena about the divorce and about Gran and all about Jan, and Lena told her that she saw *her* father for one month only in the summer, and her mother had broken her arm during the holidays, and she'd been given a new Hoola Bandoola record, which Mia could come and listen to if she came back and had dinner with them.

"But that'll be a lot of trouble if your mother's broken her arm . . . I mean—"

"Oh, my brother cooks the dinner. He always does the cooking when he's at home."

Lena shook her bushy reddish fair curls and laughed.

So they wandered arm in arm out into the square, and to add to everything the sky was blue, the snow clean and white, crunching underfoot, the sun making the big clock outside Blomströms the jeweler's glitter like gold, and giving a warm reddish summer glow to the pyramid of oranges in the big Epa store window.

So the spring term slowly got going, the spring term in which Mia's childhood definitely vanished around the corner.

Afterward Mia used to think back on that winter and spring as a kind of border country between childhood and adulthood, as the time when she slowly became aware of continuity and events which before had lain in the shadow, when she became aware of what it meant to try to understand your own and others' reactions . . . to grow into a responsibility which no one else could take for you; the time when she slowly realized—or perhaps she didn't realize it at all until much later—how the past is woven into the present, how quickly yesterday becomes today becomes tomorrow.

It was some time before everyday life for Gran began to run smoothly and naturally, before Mia stopped lying half the night with her ears cocked, listening for any unusual sounds from Gran's room, or came rushing home in the lunch hour, her heart in her mouth, to see if everything was all right. Elsa Eriksson agreed to come in every day for a while, to cook some lunch and clean up a little. That was Dad's idea, since it proved impossible to get a visiting homemaker. Gran protested, of course, that it was much too expensive, but Dad just waved that aside. In addition, it turned out that their neighbor, Mrs. Carlsson, the one who liked her radio on full blast, was delighted to come and heat up coffee and talk about the old days. It soon turned out that her father had kicked a ball around Great Gärdet with Grandad.

"I don't get a moment's peace all day," Gran said, laughing. "But I can see that she means well. And now poor Marianne doesn't have to call up in a panic every blessed evening to see if you've finished me off yet."

"It's super sitting here and talking like this in the evenings, instead of just staring at the TV," said Mia, contentedly curling up in the corner of the sofa after dinner, when she and Dad had done the dishes.

Gran nodded. "You know, when we used to read aloud in the evenings in the old days, it was such fun. Your grandfather liked reading aloud to the kids when they were small. But that wasn't all that peculiar—he practically grew up in the WEA library . . . his dad was the superintendent there. Mia, you probably don't remember that nice old yellow building beyond Miller's Hill—it was pulled down years ago."

"I didn't know that . . . I mean that Grandad's father looked after the library."

"Gustaf was marvelous at reciting things by heart— long, long sections from all those books he devoured. *The*

Three Musketeers and *Tales of an Army Surgeon* and . . ."

"What *are* you talking about?" said Dad as he came in with the coffee. "Are you telling Mia about when Father used to read aloud to us, Mom? Yes, it was exciting, when we sat around the kitchen table in old Hall Street and read *The Fortunes of Mr. Arne* so that our eyes came out of our heads."

"Why are they sharpening such long knives at Brane-hög?" intoned Gran in a voice of doom.

"Yes, good God, I remember Börje was so dead scared, he ran off and hid in the closet."

"And do you remember during the war, when we read *Ride Tonight* and got so excited!"

They went on remembering . . .

"Why didn't *you* ever read aloud to us, Dad?" said Mia accusingly.

"Well, I suppose that's something that's got neglected," said Dad slowly, pouring out another cup of coffee. "There never seemed to be time for it in a way. And then there's the TV. Nothing would stop Lillan watching TV, would it?"

"Well," said Gran, "if you live in the television age, then you live in it—and that has its good sides and bad. Children learn a lot about the world nowadays, things we had no idea about. And that's good. All those sex-and-violence rubbishy American papers they buy at the news-stands are much worse."

"Oh, but what about *Swedish Humor*?" said Dad, laughing. "Do you remember those tattered old magazines full of funny stories we had in the outside john in Håll Street? They were probably pretty awful, too."

He stubbed out his cigarette and drank down the last of his coffee.

"I must be . . ." he said, getting up.

"Do you have to go already?"

"Yes, I'm afraid I have to dash off to the leisure-activities committee . . . it's a pity. You and I haven't sat and talked like this about the old days for . . . well, for years . . . whatever the reason for that has been. But there'll be other evenings, I suppose. Bye for now."

"Gran, what was Grandad really like?" asked Mia after her father had gone. "I hardly remember him, and he was so ill, too."

To her surprise Mia saw that Gran's cheeks turned a little pink and her tone of voice was almost formal as she spoke.

"You should know, Mia, once and for all, that your grandfather was the most wonderful man in the world."

"Oh, Gran, that does sound nice—'the most wonderful man in the world'! How lovely to be able to say that."

"Yes, I was lucky."

"But tell me, why . . . I mean, in what *way* was he the most wonderful man in the world?" exclaimed Mia. "Can you tell me?"

"Yes," said Gran, staring out of the window for a long time, looking over at the Datema computer advertisement glittering against the dark blue winter sky. "Well, how shall I put it? He was so warm . . . so kind and wise, and yet strong. Well, I don't mean just physically strong— though he was that in his young days—but he had confidence in himself. And if you have that, then you can afford to be generous and indulgent toward others. And then he could laugh, you see. I think that was probably the most important thing—that we nearly always had such fun together."

"But didn't he have *any* bad characteristics? He must have."

"Oh, yes, he did that. But I loved him for those too . . . just as he accepted me with all my faults and failings."

"How good, Gran, how good that must be . . ."

They sat in silence for a long time, Gran twisting and turning her watch chain as she always did when her thoughts were wandering far away. The light from the lamp fell onto her rheumatic hands, and in the quiet room you could hear the sound of the gold chain clicking against her two gold rings.

"But, oh, what a hoopla there was before I got him, I'll have you know," she said suddenly, grimacing a little. "You can't imagine how furious my mother was."

"Oh, tell me."

So Gran told her . . .

How young Astrid Matilda Johansson from Backen in Vagnhärad came to Stockholm in the autumn of 1919 to go to school. She was to live with her uncle, who had a decorating business on Västmanna Street, and she was to help look after his five children, at the same time going to Birkagården Folk High School.

"That sounds like hard work," exclaimed Mia.

"It certainly was, but it was a dream that had to be realized. More my mother's dream than mine perhaps. Mother had had the same dream herself—to be allowed to continue school and become a teacher. She was very bright at school, and if she'd been a boy, then someone would have certainly paid for her education. But she was a girl, and so instead went into service as the maid of the province's doctor in Vagnhärad, and then she became the wife of a farmer. Soon enough she had four children, more, in fact, but two died as babies. Three boys and a girl. My brothers didn't like book work—two of them emigrated to America, anyway—and the oldest, Elof, was to take over the farm, it was always said. I was the youngest and Mother put all her hopes in me. I had good marks when I left the village school, but unfortunately that year was when the First World War broke out, and there was no question of sending a fourteen-year-old away anywhere—least of all to Stockholm, where times were bad, with food shortages and disturbances."

"But wasn't there a high school near where you lived, which you could have gone to?" asked Mia.

"That's all you know," said Gran. "High schools were only for *boys*—if girls wanted to continue in school, they had to go privately, and that cost a lot of money."

"Oh, yes, of course, that's true . . ."

"So I had to stay at home on the farm for the time being, helping in the house . . . and it wasn't always all that easy."

"Was your mother strict?"

Gran hesitated a little, seeking for words.

"Mother was a person who had difficulties with herself," she said in the end. "Her disappointment ate its way inward and made her bitter and aggressive. Especially against Father, who got the blame for most things. Well, it affected us all. Sometimes I couldn't keep my mouth shut when she was really hurtful, and then I'd get a sharp box over the ears, although I was so big. . . ."

She stopped again and sat in silence for a while.

"Then I went out and hid myself in the garden and hated her. Hitting children is dangerous—you can get hate injuries to your mind, though no one knows about them.

"When I didn't dare answer back any longer, but learned to keep quiet and accept it like the others, I began to dream. Dream about quarrels . . . when Mother hurled awful, wounding, cruel words, but words which always had enough truth in them to get through and stick. Words which you remembered for years. And her eyes—her eyes were the worst—hard, alien, desperate. Though you didn't understand the despair then, and you didn't know what to do with it.

"Afterward I did try to understand—but then it was too late. And twenty years after her death, it still happened that I dreamed that kind of hate dream about Mother—isn't that awful?"

They were both silent for a long while.

"But what happened in Stockholm, then? . . . I mean when you met Grandad and all that?"

"Yes, sorry, Mia dear. I'm being long-winded, but I would like to . . . I'd like you, too, to know something about what disappointment can do to people. Well now, Grandad. I met him during the second fall term in Stockholm. He had friends who worked for my uncle and we met after a lecture—I think it was a lecture by that women's movement bigwig, Lydia Wahlström. Or perhaps it was her sister, who ran a society called Vigilance, which was formed to protect young girls from the white-slave traffic."

"White-slave traffic! I always thought that only existed in schoolgirl stories."

"No, indeed, Mia, it was deadly earnest—lots of young girls and children were sold to brothels in those days."

"Were you already interested in things like that then—I mean, the women's movement?"

"Yes, you see, at that time it was quite natural because women had just got the vote. Nevertheless, Gustaf was my guardian the first year we were married, before the new marriage laws were passed in 1921."

"Was . . . was the husband the wife's guardian? How absolutely crazy!"

"And not just that, I'll have you know. Until then he had in fact been her *master*, a master who had the legal right to force his wife to work, whether or not she wanted to, or was able to, or had the energy to . . . have you ever heard of anything like it? And right up to the end of the thirties, the use of contraceptives was forbidden . . . it makes you gasp that it was all so recent."

"Help! Is that true? But what happened then . . . I mean after you got married—did you go on taking an interest in women's rights?"

"No, I didn't, I'm ashamed to say. Nothing much came of it later, unfortunately."

"Didn't Grandad like it?"

"On the contrary. If he hadn't, and been some kind of domestic tyrant, then I'd probably have turned uppity. No, he was very liberal when it came to things like that—helped me with the dishes and pushed the baby carriage and everything—much more than most boys did in those days. But it was just that that did it, I think. I didn't feel in the least oppressed by my husband, and so I stopped worrying about my oppressed sisters. I was happy and content, we shared our few pennies between us, we had children and worked hard, he on the railways and me at home after the children were born—it was enough for me. It was a long time afterward, really not until now in my old age, that I woke up to the fact that we women have a mutual responsibility for each other, regardless of our own situation."

"But your education—your mother's dream—what happened about that?"

"That went down the drain, of course. I quit the classes when I got engaged to Gustaf. He was several years older than me, and thought we should get married as soon as possible."

"Your poor mother."

"Yes, poor Mother. Though I didn't think that at the time. At the time, I just thought she was cruel and inhuman, not allowing me to get married. I was under age, you see, so I had to get their permission—well, only Father's in actual fact because a mother wasn't a guardian of her children then—but she forced Father to say no. If I'd at least got hold of a grander man with more money . . . but a 'station man,' as she called Gustaf, oh, no, not on your life. It sounded so snobbish and awful then, but now I understand that it wasn't snobbishness so much as boundless disappointment over my lost opportunities."

"But it must have been horrible for you."

"Yes, it was. She didn't give in until I wrote home to say I was five months pregnant."

"Were you?"

"Of course. And we got permission. But she refused to

see me. Father sometimes came up to Stockholm to see us. But I never saw Mother again until the day of Father's funeral. We managed to bring about some kind of reconciliation, so that we could meet in the future. But it was never often."

Mia sat in silence, tears in her eyes. Then she wiped them away with the back of her hand and said in a thick voice, "But, Gran, I don't understand . . . I don't see how you can sit there and talk so calmly about all this. It must have been terrible—wretchedly miserable."

Gran smiled a little. "Yes, I can see perhaps that you think it sounds a bit cold when I talk like that about Mother, but when you're as old as I am, you'll find that certain miseries become sort of mourned away—you've struggled with your hurt feelings and defiance for so long, and your guilty conscience, that they become empty shells. I don't think it would have helped if I'd gone down on my bended knees, anyway. Mother's bitterness about life itself was so profound and established, there was no way out. It was too much to ask that I should turn her dream into reality. But I think she would be happy if she could see you, Mia, today —her great-granddaughter—then she'd be able to begin hoping again."

Mia was quiet for a long time.

"But then I'd have to be careful about telling her that I thought I was pregnant about a month ago, and that my boyfriend suggested I should give up school and cook his meals for him," she said slowly, looking up at Gran with a comical grimace. "Because then she would probably have thought we women would never make any headway."

Gran smiled slightly at Mia, then leaned forward and patted her cheek.

"That was nice of you to tell me, Mia."

"I . . . I've been thinking of doing so for a long time, but then . . ."

The ringing of the telephone in the hall interrupted her.

"Järeberg."

"Hi!"

"Hi, Lena. The chemistry was a real drag today, wasn't it, but I've actually struggled my way through it. We can compare notes at break, can't we? As long as I don't have to go up to the blackboard tomorrow . . . I get hiccoughs from sheer fright if the Colt so much as looks at me. What? How lovely. Oh, super. I haven't been to a party for ages. Bosse and his friends. Fine . . . For the babies in the class . . . well, nothing wrong with them. Lots of them are sweet . . . but . . . okay, thanks a lot. And should I bring anything with me . . . sandwiches or something? Oh, so Bosse's going to do a casserole—great! But I could bring some cheese or something. Great . . . bye, then, sleep well and dream about iodides ┃ ovalent bonds. Bye!"

"Oh, Gran, ┃'e been invited to a party by Lena and her brother on Saturday. At their place."

"How nice. It's a long time since you went out to enjoy yourself, Mia dearest. You've just been sitting at home look-ing after old Gran."

"Don't be silly," said Mia, leaning forward and kissing Gran on the cheek. "Oh, Gran, you've got the softest cheeks in the world, you know—like velvet."

"That's just old age, my dear," said Gran, smiling. "Mia . . . I was thinking . . . if you don't mind my asking . . . is it all over between you and Jan?"

"Yes, practically."

"How do you mean?"

"Well, I mean we haven't had a great breakup or anything like that, but it sort of went through after the . . . how can I put it . . . the commotion when I thought I was pregnant. We sort of got so scared stiff that it drove us apart or something."

"It was fortunate things worked out as they did."

"Yes," said Mia slowly. "It's strange. It's as if you have to be terrified once first before you understand what it's really all about. What a frightful responsibility you have to take . . . not only for yourself and those nearest to you . . . well, the future, but also for a poor little kid. It's horrible. All around it's strange that you don't really understand anything until you're in the middle of it all. Like this business with Mother and Dad. Now I've really suddenly realized how important it is that . . . girls . . . women get a proper education and training and not just make a little pocket money on the side."

"Yes," said Gran. "But it's not as simple at. There are so many things that come into it. If the going to be unemployment like in the thirties, for ins ce, then the wives will no doubt have to be so kind as to go back home. Yes, and then a whole lot of psychologists and doctors say that it's never a good thing if mothers aren't at home with the children . . . and anyway what could one do when there were no day nurseries . . . hardly any kindergartens, and the ones that existed were for rich people. Everyone couldn't do what I did . . . deliver papers at night so that I could be at home with the children in the daytime."

"Speaking of that," said Mia, jumping up from the sofa,

"we've probably got to do a group project on the women's movement and sex roles and all that, you know. We've got a new young teacher—a super person, incidentally. We call her the Eight because she belongs to Group Eight, that new women's movement group. You know we read *A Doll's House* in Norwegian last term.. And last week the Eight brought her guitar with her and sang some things from a record called *Songs about Women*."

"*Sleeping Beauty has taken her valium, to soothe her aches and pains*," interrupted Gran, humming somewhat out of tune.

"What? Do *you* know something about it?"

"Old women listen to the radio, so even they catch a glimpse of what's going on."

"You really are super, Gran," exclaimed Mia, flying over and hugging her from behind. "You really are."

"Well, this super oldie must now go to bed so that she doesn't become superfluous. It'll be ten o'clock soon. Give me my stick, will you, and then I think I'll celebrate with a bottle of mineral water if you'd get one out of the refrigerator for me."

"You know, if we could have our group work meeting here one evening, then you could join in and help, as you know such a lot . . . if you think you could manage that . . . ?"

"That'd be 'super,'" said Gran, smiling and placing the end of her stick on the floor.

Mia stayed sitting on the little folding seat in the elevator for a long time before bringing herself to press the button up to her floor. She was in such a fantastically good mood.

It had been a perfect evening at Lena's and Bosse's. Mia could hardly remember ever having been to such a completely successful party.

Actually she'd hardly ever been to that kind of party before, with so many older people. At her old school they had mostly mixed with their school contemporaries. That time she had met Jan had been sheer chance; he was a friend of someone's older brother, who'd come by accident.

But this evening she and Lena had been the only two still at school, the others were either college students or working. Bosse was going to be a nursery-school teacher and was doing his practice teaching at a nursery school, another was earning pocket money as a bus driver, some were training as social workers, and one girl was actually at the veterinary college . . . and then Martin, who was studying music.

Martin. Mia sat and soaked up the name. God, he was beautiful.

Beautiful large mouth and lots of white teeth.

His good-night kiss had not really gone yet. She lifted her hand and felt. At that moment she caught sight of herself in the narrow elevator mirror and grinned happily at her flushed face and shining eyes.

And what good food.

And what great talk.

And what lovely music.

Though—of course, she would never meet him again. A guy like that naturally had hordes of girls after him. And yet he had danced most with her.

No, for heaven's sake, someone was coming into the entrance hall—she'd better press the button . . . *And shall we play for the weak ones, shall we play for the small,* she hummed softly as the elevator whizzed up and stopped with a jerk on the seventh floor.

Then it was a matter of not waking Gran and Dad. Mia took off her boots on the doormat and crept into the kitchen with them in her hand. It wasn't worth beginning to mess about with coat hangers, which had a way of crashing down on the floor so that the place echoed.

At once she saw that the light was on in Gran's room. The door was just ajar.

"Mia, are . . . is that . . . you?"

Gran's voice sounded like a rattling whisper.

In a second Mia was at the door.

"Oh, Mia . . . how good that . . . that you . . ."

"Are you all right?" exclaimed Mia, rushing over to the bed.

Idiotic question.

"My pills," whispered Gran, pressing her right arm round her left shoulder. "Oh, it hurts so. . . . I dropped . . . the bottle . . . when I . . ."

"Where, Gran . . . are these them?" Mia's hands were shaking so much that she could hardly pick the pills up off the floor. "Here, Gran . . . I'll get a glass of whisky . . . you know that's what the doctor said we could do . . . it works more quickly then . . . wait . . ."

"It's all right . . . all right, Mia. Don't . . . don't worry." Gran groaned, pressing her right arm even harder against her chest. Her face was so white . . . white as paper, a whiteness Mia had never seen in her life before.

Mia knelt down on the floor by the bed and held Gran's other hand between her own. The pain in her chest and down her back and arm was making Gran twist her body as if she had a cramp.

"Why didn't you call Dad?"

"I did, but . . . he didn't . . . hear . . . or, Mia . . . hold on hard . . . it hurts right out to my teeth."

Oh, dear God, do something, thought Mia. Supposing she dies. She feels like a little bird about to break. Aloud she tried to comfort Gran. "It'll soon pass . . . it's sure to . . . the doctor said . . . I'll put a pillow here behind your back, so you can breathe more easily."

An eternity seemed to go by, though in fact it was no more than about a minute before the attack began to decline. The groaning grew weaker, and although Gran's chest was still rising and falling jerkily, Mia saw her cheeks were slightly less white.

"Do you want me to get Dad?" asked Mia.

"Oh . . . no," Gran panted, trying to smile. "Men are just a nuisance."

"But the doctor . . . Gran . . . perhaps he should come?"

"In the middle . . . of the . . . night, heavens . . . no . . . I'm . . . not dying yet. But it would be . . . nice . . . if you'd sit here for . . . a while with me . . . until things calm . . . down . . ."

"Of course, Gran dear, I'll sit here on the edge of the bed and hold your hand. It's fine like this . . . wouldn't you like another sip of whisky . . . and I'll move the pillows a little lower down. There won't be any more attacks now."

So they sat in silence, and Mia held the twisted old hand in her big strong one and felt through the skin and nerves how the pain receded and Gran's breathing became more normal. With her other hand she took a handkerchief and carefully wiped away the cold sweat that had run down her face, making it shiny and sticky.

Strange that you act almost mechanically, that you're not so scared stiff that you just stand and stare or begin to cry. But Doctor Persson had said that Gran might have these sudden attacks ... if she was overwrought or upset or something.

But why just tonight in particular, when Dad and she were to have had such a quiet, peaceful Saturday evening together? Could they have quarreled? Or perhaps something had happened or someone had telephoned? Gran was very worried about Uncle Börje, who was a missionary doctor somewhere in Africa, and she'd had a letter telling her that he had jaundice.

Was she asleep now? No, the grip on her hand hadn't lessened.

"Go to bed now ... Mia dear ...," whispered Gran, opening her eyes. "You must be ... terribly tired."

"I'm not a bit tired, Gran. In fact I'm very much awake."

"Did ... you have ... a good time?"

"Yes, marvelous."

Gran closed her eyes again and Mia sat looking at her protruding eyelids, which lay like violet bowls against the pale skin, at the dark circles under her eyes, and at all the fine little smile wrinkles stretching out toward her temples. The strong straight nose and firm mouth gave her face the stern look Mia remembered from childhood and which had always scared her a little. She suddenly saw how like Dad Gran was, too, and when she raised her head and looked at her own distant reflection in the mirror above the chest of drawers, she also saw how she herself was like them both.

It filled her with a strange mixture of joy and anxiety. When she looked down again, she saw that Gran was lying there with her eyes wide open.

"It's funny," she said, her voice sounding much firmer. "When an attack is over, you feel . . . almost exhilarated."

"Shall I make some tea . . . I feel just like a cup of tea," said Mia, getting up to pick up her coat that she had flung down on a chair.

"Yes, that would be good . . . if you've got the energy."

And so it came about that as the late winter dawn fought against the night darkness above the sleeping inhabitants of their building, and the reassuring clock in the concrete church struck both five and six, Mia sat on the edge of Gran's bed and drank tea and ate cinnamon rusks and talked about death.

"You are kind, Mia, letting me talk on without interrupting me or putting me off with, 'You'll go on for years yet.' . . . People don't seem able to accept that an old person wants to talk about his or her death. Do you really think that we old people live with our eyes shut . . . never facing anything?"

"One's so afraid . . . so afraid oneself . . . that one really can't endure it," replied Mia slowly. "One doesn't want to think about it." She was sitting curled up on the bedside rug with Gran's crocheted shawl around her shoulders. "And then you don't know . . . what to say. You're not used to it really."

"Yes, death has become something shameful, an unsuitable subject to talk about nowadays. People don't live so close to it as they did in the old days. People die in hospitals, are kept alive at all costs, but they haven't got anyone to sit by their bedside and listen to their agony, least of all their relatives, who get frightened and hardly dare visit. Last month an old woman died at the Home. They sent for her children, but they didn't come. Of course the staff is nice and kind, and you get all the nursing and injections you need—but you need something for your poor soul, too . . . not pity . . . just a little sympathetic insight."

"Are you afraid of dying, Gran?" Mia asked gently.

"Not now. But before . . . then it was an incomprehensible terror. Gustaf was never afraid, strangely enough. We often talked about death and that helped me." She was silent for a while. "Though it's annoying not to be able to know what happens."

Mia smiled slightly. "I've got a book about a young girl who finds out that she's going to die of leukemia . . . she writes a letter and tries to say what she feels . . . she thought that was the worst thing of all—not being able to know how things go, just to be allowed to stick your head into the world and sniff at it a little and then out again . . .'

Gran nodded.

"There's a poem about death in that book, too, which is great," Mia went on. "How does it go now?

> "Death is only the bramble
> round pellucid blooms
> the dark jewel
> that offers admission to the feast."

"The dark jewel that offers admission to the feast—that's beautiful," murmured Gran. "But now I think I'll try and get a little sleep. Look, the sun's already rising. Go to bed now, and sleep well, Mia darling, and thank you for tonight."

Mia stood by the window for a while, watching the red morning glow spreading over the high-school roof. She was tired but calm.

Before she undressed, she wrote a note to Dad on a piece of paper on the kitchen table, telling him what had happened. When she woke up at about two o'clock, the doctor had already been there, and lunch was on the table.

"Why didn't you wake me up?" Dad asked slightly reproachfully, stroking Mia's tousled hair.

"Gran didn't want me to. What did the doctor say?"

"That she's to stay in bed and rest for a few days . . . otherwise nothing special. Were you very scared, Mia love?"

"I . . . I don't know. I didn't seem to have time. And then it was good when the attack was over . . . we had tea and talked about death."

Her father frowned, looking uncomfortable.

"That was a bit unsuitable, wasn't it?"

"Why? Gran wanted to. Old people like talking about death."

Mia didn't remember until long into the afternoon that she had fallen in love. With Martin. Martin with his long fair angel hair and Beatle mustache. Martin who was so lively and nice. And marvelous at the piano. Martin who had danced with almost no one else but Mia the whole evening.

Though of course he wouldn't get in touch with her.

Lots of work to do. And lots of girls in tow, for sure.

That evening she would have to write to Mother.

$\mathcal{M}$IA was on the train going back to Stockholm, staring absently out the window. She had been to stay for the midterm holiday with Grandpa and Granny in Åsa, to see Mother and Lillan.

They had been six confusing days.

Mia didn't know whether she was tired or rested, happy or miserable. Her mind was a wasp's nest of thoughts that kept buzzing about. She was longing to get back home to Dad and Gran and her own bed, and yet the parting with Mother on the station in Gothenburg was like a stinging wound in her heart.

The compartment was crowded with people: families going home after the holiday, kids pushing and bickering about Superman comics, chattering about sandwiches and chewing gum, and babies dropping their pacifiers under the seats. There was a smell of rubber boots, salami, and fruit chews. An old woman with cotton wool in her ears was sitting opposite Mia by the window, reading *The War Cry*.

Mia crept deeper into her coat, which was hanging on a hook in the corner, trying to hide herself in it like a tent, to shut out the outside world.

Outside the train window a radiant spring day raced past.

The lakes outside Alinsås lay like shiny ice rinks with borders of green pines and purple birches. Bare yellow fields, snowdrifts on the north side, muddy roads, dark blue mountain ridges in the distance, train stations, white, yellow, and brick-red water towers and white churches, telephone wires that rose and fell. Everything rushed by Mia's unseeing eyes beneath a blue sky playing at being April rather than February.

Mia ate a banana.

Everything was such hard work.

First it had been such hard work getting away, arranging with a retired district nurse to come and live with Gran for the week. Mother insisted on Mia's coming down for the holiday and, of course, she wanted to. But then her mother thought that Gran should go back to the Home before she had another heart attack. She thought they had experimented enough, she said. Mia was in despair. But Dad came down on her side and worked like a demon to find someone who would come and live in.

It actually seemed that he didn't do it just for Mia's sake. Once, when just the two of them were there, Dad suddenly stroked Mia's cheek and said a little shyly and awkwardly, "You know, Mia, that was a very good idea of yours to ask Gran to come and live here with us. It looks as if we're really going to get to know each other at last . . . and I think Gran has blossomed, don't you? She's quite changed."

Yes, heavens, it had been a hectic time before she got away, and all the time she'd gone around with her ears cocked, waiting for that darned telephone to ring! For Martin to get in touch, as he said he would that evening.

"Has anyone phoned?" she asked, every time she came through the front door. And Gran shook her head and sighed.

"Ah, me," she said. "I wonder if there will ever be such equality between the sexes so that a girl can call up a boy and make a date. Just think, after all these years—the same eternal waiting for the noble male to condescend to stretch out his hand and graciously call the patiently waiting maiden to his side . . ."

"Hey!" Mia laughed. But it was true, at least in her case.

Of course he called the day before Mia was to leave and invited her to a concert on Sunday evening.

Damn and blast it. Mia could hardly control her voice on the telephone. "I'm afraid . . ."

Typical, wasn't it?

"Okay, then I'll call again another time."

Of course it had been nice in Åsa, and her eighteenth birthday was festive with lots of presents.

But since Lillan was having her midterm holiday later and Mother was working during the day, Mia stayed with Granny in the kitchen most of the time or went for walks with Grandpa and the dogs along the shore. Of course it had been wonderful, even if perhaps not so much Grandpa but Granny anyway talked incessantly. They were awfully nice. She was served morning coffee every day, and Granny baked pies and cakes in her honor, even when it wasn't her birthday. She must eat up, poor child . . .

Of course, it had been nice.

And yet she lived through the whole time in some kind of state of unpleasant tension. It was strangely difficult to see Mother again, and their first meeting on the platform came as a surprise in itself. All her loss had welled up and almost stuck in her throat, thickening in her chest. For the first few minutes, they just stood there holding on to each other, the tears pouring down. *Oh, Mother.*

So unnatural that they had left each other.

It hurt, but was nice at the same time.

But then gradually, quite soon, something else came. They examined each other, seeking suspiciously for changes. "You look pale and thin, Mia." "You look marvelous, Mother, a new hairdo . . . it suits you."

There was an invisible wall. Does that really happen so quickly? Even though you love each other?

There was, for instance, Mother not wanting to talk about Gran. She was still saying it was irresponsible. Suddenly Mia realized that it was all a kind of jealousy, and then she couldn't even expound on how nice it was with the three of them at home.

Then when Mother began to talk enthusiastically about her new job, her good boss, and all the nice people at work and how well Lillan was doing at school, it was Mia's turn to be jealous.

Lillan, too, was hard to approach, after the first stormy hugs of welcome. She just talked about her own things . . . her riding and new friends and about films on television that Mia hadn't seen.

Mia went around in a state of indefinable disappointment all the time, in herself and in them.

Then there was that man who telephoned and asked after Mother one afternoon, when Mia was alone at the house. He clearly thought she was Mother, as they spoke so alike. "Hello, darling," he said in that hearty accent. "What about this evening?"

It wasn't necessarily anything, of course, it wasn't necessarily anything, but all the same. Already. After such a short time.

But Mother couldn't help it that men were attracted by

her. She looked so very pretty and young. And anyway ...

In that case—all this "trial separation," as they called it, was it already too late? That "trial" had become almost a defense against worrying about the future. It hadn't seemed worthwhile beginning to worry about it yet. Was that barrier already torn down—was Mother already on her way out of Mia's life ... and Dad's? Was it just talk so that it all wouldn't seem so brutal?

But she herself? She would soon be adult and moving away from both Mother and Dad. Soon. Yes, soon, but not soon enough.

Mother hadn't said anything about it. But, of course, there was probably nothing to talk about.

There hadn't really been much chance to talk together on their own, as Mia had hoped. On Mother's afternoon off, they went out for a walk, and they had a short time together on the last evening. Mother asked if Jan had come back. Mia told her that she'd recently had a postcard. An "I'm-very-well-how-are-you" postcard. For a moment it shot through Mia's head that she should tell her all about that experience with her overdue period; it was awful in some way to have been part of something so important without Mother having the slightest idea about it.

"I've often—"

"Oh, yes, now I come to think of it, Mia," interrupted Mother, "I hope you've fixed things up—you know, what we talked about at Christmas?"

"Oh, yes, I had an appointment with the gynecologist just before I came down."

"Well?"

"Well, he was actually a really nice doctor, and also he

took his time, so you weren't rushed. The examination was nothing anyway ... some girls go on and on about it. At first he told me all about the different methods and side effects and all that. And then he asked me a little cautiously whether I had a fiancé or a steady boyfriend or whether I slept around. He did tell me you had to be careful whatever method you used."

"I'm glad you've fixed that, anyway, darling," said Mother. "So that you don't fall by the wayside like Barbro."

"Oh, she was shining like the sun itself in her bridal attire, I'll have you know," replied Mia. "I was at the church and watched the whole performance ... gold crown and white lace and lilies of the valley! And her mother-in-law in tears and mink tails ... Aunt Elsa actually looked more in control."

"Yes, good heavens, you can understand that."

"Then there was the reception at Barbro's with tiny sandwiches and gateau and lots of relations. I presented them with an oven-proof dish, as I missed the engagement party. And the bride had to go out and be sick in the middle of her father-in-law's speech."

"And then, no doubt, the bridal pair left for the sunny South ..."

"Yes, for Örebro."

At that moment Granny had called out that dinner would soon be ready, and there was no more just-us-two talk.

The train thundered on.

More patchy fields, more birch glades, more pewter-colored lakes, more railway yards with their mess of tracks and wires, more kids chattering about candies and going to the bathroom . . .

Mia ate Granny's cold wafer pancakes.

Dusk fell and swept mild pinkish-gray veils over the countryside, and houses turned on golden button eyes. When the train stopped in Katrineholm, Mia was asleep behind her coat curtain. Just before she fell asleep, she thought with a twinge of conscience about how scornfully she had described Barbro's wedding to Mother—Barbro, who had once been her best friend.

"Are you coming with me this afternoon to celebrate the spring?" Lena had scribbled on the back of a mimeographed sheet, pushing it over to Mia toward the end of the last lesson on Friday.

"Sure! How shall we celebrate it?" Mia whispered back.

"Go to a café . . . buy blouses . . . get our hair cut. I've got lots of money. I had a job over the holiday."

"Oh, yes, I want to go and find a coat, too. Mother gave me money for my birthday, and I saw a fantastic corduroy trench coat in Hers yesterday."

It had been a slow dull week since Mia had got back from Halland. Gran was tired and had a cold and Dad was cross about some fuss at work. The fine spring weather had reverted to foggy, dirty winter, with low clouds and outbreaks of influenza. Martin hadn't called.

But today, Friday, spring had come back just as suddenly as it had disappeared. The wind was mild, the snowdrops reappeared, Dad hummed in the bathroom, you forgot to button up your jacket, and the sunlight danced in the

City Hall's many windows, making it look like a crystal palace.

The math teacher was in a good mood and praised everyone.

The principal excused the whole school from the last class because . . . because of something.

Full to the brim with The Corner's freshly baked pastries and chocolate goodies, Mia and Lena wandered around the store trying on things. Not just blouses and coats, but everything that came their way . . . jackets, skirts, sweaters, suits in beige, red, black, marine blue. "The Wonderful Forties," it said in pale green garlands above it all.

"My mother went quite crazy when she saw that gauze hats were coming back," said Lena, jamming a pink beret onto her red curls. "And she's not exactly a fashion plate otherwise. But she had a fantastic fluffy gauze hat when she got engaged in nineteen forty-seven, and she never forgets that."

"The Eight should see us now," giggled Mia, holding a long-skirted silk jersey dress against herself. "Femininity is blossoming this spring."

"Well, the Eight was wearing sexy new corduroy jeans yesterday, so I don't think she's one of those who take the line that just because you fight for the women's movement, you can't be smartly dressed. I think that's dead stupid . . . the boys can be as smart as they like nowadays, if they want to, so why shouldn't we also do the best we can."

"They mean we shouldn't spend all day standing in front of the mirror. 'Don't spend unnecessary time on your appearance,' it said in that book on sisterhood which I've just plowed through for our group work—it's good, actually, but, Lord, it sounds like hard work."

"Yes, you begin to see that lots and lots of women have *preferred* to stay at home and be kept and oppressed instead of going out and competing in the employment market and in politics."

"It's unfair to blame all oppression on men."

"But we've probably been so beaten into the ground that we haven't dared or had the energy to rise up. Do you think I should take this blouse? Or is the green one nicer?"

With Lena's new green blouse in a bag and with the change from a blue trench coat for Mia, the girls swept on through the shopping center in their celebration of spring.

"Wait for me while I get my hair cut," said Lena. "It won't take long. And you can give advice. I always go crazy when one of those determined guys starts ravaging with his scissors. Why don't you get yours cut, too? . . . It must get awfully hot with all that hair hanging around your neck. And everyone seems to have had a center part for ages now. Just think how great it'd be with those bangs that are combed up at the ends, you know, like Bosse's Anna . . . and then short around the ears, Mia. Or one of those short nineteen-forties styles with great waves . . . that'd really take the cake . . . like an old film star."

"Don't be crazy. Anyway, no one would be free in a hairdresser's at this time on a Friday afternoon."

A last-minute cancelation just as the two girls stepped into Marguerite's on the second floor at Domus decided Mia.

"Is there by any chance anyone free to cut my friend's

hair?" said Lena in her usual self-confident radiant way. "She wants to be a new woman."

"Oh, you're crazy," wailed Mia, and the next moment she was sitting in a chair with a violet-colored plastic gown around her shoulders. "But not short," she said hastily, wrapping her arm around her long brown mane of hair.

"Perhaps bangs and a ponytail," said Miss Bojan, combing Mia's hair out at random. "Your hair would look fine with bangs combed upward at the ends . . . it falls well . . . and then swept back at the sides and a ponytail at the back of the neck. It's to be drawn back at the sides this year, they say in Paris."

"There you are," said Lena, thrusting her cheerful curly head around the mirror. "If *Paris* says so, then you *can't* resist it, can you?"

That was how it happened that half an hour later Mia stepped out into the square as "quite a new woman," with Lena dancing ecstatically alongside her.

"You look absolutely fantastic, Mia, can't you see? Smart and fabulously adult in some way. Look in that shop window."

So Mia looked in every shop window in the shopping center to get used to this new girl who was her. Lena was right; it suited her. And it was nice with something new. A little impractical, of course, to have to keep bangs in order, instead of having a center part, which was so simple, but all the same . . . and it felt marvelous to have her hair brushed away from her ears and neck.

"You look like . . . who is it you look like?"

"Elizabeth Taylor, of course," came Bosse's voice from behind them, and Lena and Mia turned quickly around.

There was Bosse laughing, with an Easter bunch of twigs sprinkled with colored feathers in his hand. Behind him stood . . . Martin.

Mia saw at once from his expression that he approved of the "new woman."

"Well, here you are," he said hastily. "And I who've been calling you up all this time. Did you have a good half term?"

"Fine, thanks," said Mia, knowing that he was lying about those calls, but not caring. She just saw his wide smile and his confident blue eyes. Her underlying infatuation rose like a balloon, a happy red balloon, shimmering in the sunlight.

"Are you coming with us to the Music Café tonight?" said Bosse. "One of Martin's buddies is playing in the band. Then we could go back home to our place and have a beer, couldn't we, Lena, as Mom's away?"

"That depends on whether Dad's home this evening," said Mia, hesitantly, not daring to admit to the joyous thumping in her chest. "Otherwise I can't leave Gran."

"Oh," said Lena, "surely your neighbor person could come if the worst comes to the worst. Try and fix it, anyway. It's said to be a fantastic band. Hurry home now, and then phone back."

$\mathcal{M}$IA and Martin were standing with their arms around each other outside the entrance to Lena's apartment building. It was cold and the stars were out, but the taste of spring was still in the air.

It had been a fantastic evening, first at the Music Café with the Banging Band—crowds of people and a huge success. Toward the end Martin had leaped in and played the piano and the audience had roared; then they had taken a gang with them and gone back to Lena and Bosse's for beer and dancing.

Mia's cheeks were burning and her head was tired from all the noise, her heart pounding with a strange excitement that had been there a long time, almost all the evening, almost since the moment she had met Martin in the square.

Thoughts had been there . . . thoughts that she hadn't even wanted to face; the knowledge of how the evening would end. They had sat on the sofa in Lena's room, their arms around each other, Mia feeling the ardor of his hands, feeling it within herself, quite a different ardor.

"Uhuh," said Martin, brushing his long hair away from his face as he kissed the tip of her nose. "Do we go back to my place or yours?"

"You know quite well we can't go to my place."

"Hell, no, of course not. I forgot you'd got the place full of oldies. Well, then, it'll have to be back to my place, then, though you'll have to excuse the mess there. I haven't had time to clean up all week, but there's always a bottle of wine, anyway . . ."

He took her by the arm and swung her along down toward the bus stop.

"If we hurry, we'll just catch the last bus from town."

It was the confidence in his voice that suddenly brought Mia up short. The minute before, no, seconds before, she had thought she was going to go with him, that that was what she wanted. Her heart thundered in her ears, her mouth turning quite dry. With a jerk she dug her heels in and stopped him. He turned his head and stared at her in surprise.

"Hell, come on, we have to hurry," he said impatiently.

"But listen, Martin. I can't." Mia heard herself panting. "I can't be out that long. Our neighbor was coming in to check before she went to bed, but wait . . . Dad's out at a party, you see. I'd forgotten that before, and he isn't going to be back until very late and then . . . then she'll be alone for so long and . . . you know, she's got a bad heart . . ."

The words tumbled out of her.

Martin stopped for a moment, dropping his hold on her so roughly that she staggered.

"Then you'll excuse me if I run for the bus myself," he said, pouting like a sulky child. "Hell of a shame, really . . . but bye, and thanks for this evening . . . you'll find your way back, won't you? Here's that damned bus . . . bye!"

Mia stood on the pavement, watching him racing away, his coat flapping.

"I must be crazy," she whispered. "What on earth's the matter with me? Dad isn't at a party at all. I like him, don't I? And I can cope now, can't I?"

She half ran back along the deserted street. The puddles were frozen and slippery, an empty beer can rolled in front of her feet, and the church clock struck twelve thin and comforting notes. But it wasn't comforting that Mia needed now.

"Thanks for Friday. It was great," said Mia, when she and Lena met at school on Monday.

"Yes, it was a great evening in the end, wasn't it?" Lena

laughed. "Did you go on to Martin's place afterward?"

"No, I went straight home, actually. I was awfully tired and it was pretty late."

"Gosh, yes, I was exhausted, too," said Lena easily. "And poor Martin, who was to fly to Vienna with the college on Saturday."

"Was he going to do that?"

"Yes, didn't you know? The music college has a study visit on there this week."

"Oh, really . . . no, I didn't know that. We parted somewhat hastily, actually," said Mia, a little carelessly, making a face.

"Was he angry?"

"I don't know . . . presumably . . . so I probably won't have the honor again."

"You never know with men. But you like him, don't you? It seemed so anyway on Friday."

"I don't really know . . ."

"When Mia and Lena care to finish their interesting conversation, perhaps we can begin the day's lesson," interrrupted their English teacher. "Mia can start by reading aloud from the top of page fifty-seven."

"We're thinking of meeting to discuss our group work on Friday evening," Mia said to Gran when she got back that afternoon. "It'd be great if you'd like to join in, if you can manage, that is . . . for a while, at least?"

"I'd like to very much, of course, but what do your friends think—wouldn't they be embarrassed with an old grandmother present?"

"On the contrary, they think it's a great idea. I told

them about that business of Grandad being your 'master' the first year of your marriage, and they think it'd be great if you could help. But I warn you, it gets pretty heated, because we've got quite different views. The first time we met, there was a hell of a row."

"Oh, I think I can cope with that . . . how many are you?"

"Three girls and two boys, apart from me . . . actually, there are only four girls in the whole class."

"*Four* girls in the whole class? How did that come about?"

"Well, you know, it's the technical track . . . and that's a boys' course. Most parent apparently advise girls against the technical track . . . they think it just leads to a lot of dirty and dangerous jobs. The girls in my old class thought I was crazy when I chose the technical track . . . but Mother stood up for me. She thinks I should do something in the construction industry line or something like that. But I don't know. It seems that there are quite a number of other interesting things to be. That telecommunications lab at school is fantastic, you know. I had no idea. The funny thing is that you need lower marks to get into the technical track than into the social-studies track."

"What? I didn't know that. But then perhaps things will change a bit in the end, when it comes to choosing occupations and to sex roles. I read that a lot of boys choose social-service jobs nowadays. My old friend Hulda Johansson, who was in the hospital last winter with her gallstones— she nearly fainted when a young man came in with the bed-pan, but then she was *so* delighted and maintained that he was the nicest of all the ward orderlies, so I suppose it's a matter of what you're used to."

"Yes, Lena's brother, Bosse, is going to be a nursery-school teacher, and the kids at the day nursery love him."

"To jump from one thing to another, aren't you going to offer your friends anything when they come on Friday?"

"Yes, I thought we'd have beer and sandwiches and soft drinks and potato chips and that kind of thing beforehand . . . and they'll bring stuff with them."

"If you help me a bit, perhaps I could make some of my special toffee, you know, the kind with almonds that you like."

"Great . . . it's ages since any toffee was made in this house."

"And perhaps I could read a bit from a book the librarian brought me yesterday. *Girls Should Be Like This*—it's really dreadful. Just listen to what they said a hundred years ago: *Just as a man always looks foolish with a sewing frame or embroidery, a woman also seems unfeminine and foolish at men's occupations.* Huh, no girls in the tele-laboratory then, no, indeed."

"What fun . . . you can read some of that and we can copy out the juicy bits," said Mia.

Hope it'll be a successful evening, thought Mia a little nervously, as she stood spreading sandwiches in the kitchen on Friday afternoon. It was the first time she'd asked friends from her new class back home, and she knew most of them only slightly, even if they had met a few times and talked about the planning of their group work. As long as it wasn't all too much for Gran. They were to practice those songs, too.

Suddenly Mia longed intensely for the past; for those

last years in their old home, with the old gang who came in and out and had cocoa at the kitchen table and played ball games on the field; when Dad had his old job still and Mother was at home looking after Lillan; when you thought they were happy and contented. When you saved up for a tape recorder and taped the Festival of Song and nearly died of mortification when Sweden came second from last. When Barbro and she secretly went to the forbidden *Bonnie and Clyde* film and cried the whole evening afterward.

It seemed an eternity ago now, and yet it was only a few years ago. It was horrible that things went so quickly, because you didn't seem to be able to keep up. You didn't know who you were . . . or who you should be.

It seemed as if every day had become in some way so meaningful. You found out lots of things that you didn't really know what to do with. One moment you felt safe and happy and almost grown-up, and the next moment you longed terribly for Mother and you just wanted to cry. Perhaps she was a late developer . . . the other girls all seemed so confident. When she thought now about how she had behaved last fall, the time when she had thought she was pregnant, she considered she had behaved more than just foolishly . . . but then you are what you are, aren't you?

The time since Christmas; so much had happened. It was great with Gran. She felt she herself had been almost transfomed . . . had matured . . . was growing up. And then suddenly you fell into a pit again and everything became worrisome and stupid; this strange inexplicable thing that was happening to Mother . . . drifting away somehow . . .

and then all that about the future. What would the future be like? The Easter holidays alone were a problem. Who would go and see whom and what would happen to Gran? Was she to be just shoved back into her little cell at the Home? Here you are . . . you're not needed any longer.

Mia was standing with a half-spread sandwich in her hand, staring out of the window, where the capricious March wind had suddenly begun to blow light snowflakes about, although the sun was still shining. The radio in Mrs. Carlsson's place was playing "Waterloo." Mia sighed deeply, as if to lift all the anxiety that was weighing her down.

And then there was this business of Martin.

It was so idiotic.

She knew what he was like . . . one of those guys whom all the girls fell for. Last Monday she had been all set to say no, if he had called up again after returning from Vienna, but yesterday she had seen him on the bus—he had leaned forward and waved and grinned his wide happy grin. And then—bang—the same silly old heartbeats. She had even *blushed* all by herself on the pavement—fatuous idiot!

"Oh, there's the doorbell. Are they here already?"

Mia flung the last salami sandwich into its place, popped a leftover piece of pickle into her mouth, and ran to open the door.

The toffee was in large bowls on the living-room table, and Gran was sitting in her place in her big armchair when the "sex roles gang" filed in with their paper bags and bottles and two guitars.

"Heavens, what a marvelous smell . . . is it toffee?"

"Well, folks, this is Gran," said Mia, looking with satisfaction at the cherry-red dress Gran had put on in their honor. It suited her almost better than her blue corduroy housecoat. The red color made her cheeks slightly pink and her bangs shimmered silver white and newly washed above the clear young eyes. Mia was proud that Gran was so pretty.

"I'd better introduce them to you properly, Gran," she said, "so that you know who is who. Well, Lena you've met before, and this is Lotta, who knows more about all this than any of us, because her mother's a journalist and writes about women's questions in her paper, and she herself is going to be a supervisor in some technical industry, so that's that. And she can sing, too."

A small, slim dark girl, with bangs and wearing a yellow polo shirt, stepped forward with her guitar in her hand.

"And this is our leader of the opposition, Håkan," Mia went on, pointing to a short, broad-shouldered boy with fair hair and glasses. "He thinks all this talk about sex roles is damned silly and he wants to marry a girl who stays at home and bakes and mends his underpants—"

"Hey, lay off. I mean, good evening."

"And here's his opposite—Per. He's going to be a conscientious objector and a homebody. He makes his own clothes and also plays the guitar."

A tall boy with long, newly washed hair and a shy smile bowed his way over to Gran and shook her hand.

"And last is Blondie, or Ulla, which is her proper name. She's the one who keeps order among us all and is our 'secretary' because she's so good at writing. Otherwise, she rides a motorbike and is the district swimming champion. Uhuh . . . that's that and please take a seat, all of you, and help yourselves . . . Gran made the toffee."

"Oh, really? I thought your dad must have done it," said Håkan swiftly, with a wry smile.

Everyone laughed. "That was indeed an appropriate start to a debate on sex roles," said Gran, smiling and taking a sip of her mineral water.

"Though I don't see how we're going to be able to discuss anything with all this lovely sticky toffee in our mouths," muttered Lena, popping another piece into her mouth.

"Gran, you don't eat toffee, so couldn't you begin by reading something out of that book you talked about before —what was it called now? *Girls Should Be Like This?*"

"All right," said Gran, leafing through a beautifully illustrated book she had on her knee. "There's a great deal of edifying stuff to choose from here. And the pictures are not uninteresting, either. I'll pass it around later. I can start with this nice sentence from an etiquette book from 1844: *Obedience, so necessary to everyone, is especially necessary to a woman.* Or this: *What knowledge is necessary for a girl's upbringing then? None other than such that will cultivate her understanding of becoming a reasonable person. To what purpose will she then put her cultivated reasonableness. To domestic happiness in the future.*"

"Hell."

"And listen to what girls were to occupy themselves with —well, this concerns so-called nice girls, of course, 'of good character and breeding' as it was called. *Adorn a woman well if she is practiced in the following exercises: Dancing. Singing. Playing the lute, flute, or pianoforte. Drawing.*

Lacquering. Embroidery. Making wax fruit. Cutting and patching, folding table napkins, etc. Such exercises will both entertain and be of gain to her."

"What rubbish . . ."

"And people agreed to that . . . ?"

"It's not all that odd then, that it's taken so darned long for the women's movement to get going," said Lotta. "*Cutting and patching!* Jesus, hold me up! Pass me a toffee."

"No, now we must get organized and try to get some order into all this," cried Ulla, waving her pen and paper about. "Before we get so drunk on toffee that we just sit and groan. Shall we begin by practicing a song, or what? Which ones are we going to include, anyway?"

"I think we should have that 'A Nurse I'm Going to Be, Tarara-fiddlededee,'" said Lena. "It's so marvelously awful . . ."

"And then 'Small Voices' or whatever it's called—it's got such a fantastic tune. We can sing that as an introductory song, I think," said Per.

"Yes, and then we'll bring in some of those telling statistics—that always makes an impression. For instance: women make up fifty-one per cent of all votes. In Parliament: twenty-one per cent women. In County Councils: nineteen per cent women. In Local Councils: eighteen per cent women . . ."

"Is it really that low?" said Håkan doubtingly.

"It is that low, my good sir," said Lena. "Do you want to hear some more? In public schools there are about seventy-five thousand teachers, two-thirds of them women. Ninety-six per cent of all promotions go to approximately twenty-five thousand male teachers . . ."

"Yes, and I've got some good figures here, too," said Per.

"From that report on lower income groups. Of all the full-time employees, forty-one-point-four per cent of women come into the lower income bracket and only nine per cent of the men!"

"That's amazing—crazy!"

"Have you divided up the tasks, then, or how have you done all this?" asked Gran.

"Yes, that's it," said Ulla. "Someone has collected all those idiotic slogans and drawings in ads, and some have read books or plowed through the women's magazines and articles on sex roles and all that sort of thing."

"And heavens above, we've found some hair-raising things; you'd hardly believe it," sighed Mia.

"But now it's a matter of getting it all into some kind of shape," said Ulla in a troubled voice. "There's such a hell of a lot, and you don't really know how . . . or where . . ."

There was a pause and everyone sat leafing through notes and newspaper clippings.

"How did the ice hockey go?" whispered Håkan.

"Four–one for us," Ulla whispered back.

"Great . . ."

"Let's have a song," said Per, "so that we get into the right mood."

"That'd be fun," said Gran, "because I must go after that. I usually go to bed quite early."

Per and Lotta began to tune their guitars.

"Shall we sing 'Voices'?"

"What pitch?"

"Not too high . . ."

> *"Why do girls have such small voices?*
> *Why are girls so hard to hear?*

What does a girl who wants to speak do
When everyone round her shouts?
WHAT'S SHE WHISPERING?
WE CAN'T HEAR!
SPEAK A LITTLE LOUDER!
Should a girl sit quietly
And just hope and pray
That a boy will say
What she was thinking?
Or should she get up
And yell
IF YOU'D ONLY KEEP QUIET
AND LISTEN
I'D TELL
Then you'd hear what I want to say?
Oh, giiiirrrrls
Oh, giiiirrrrls
We must raise our voices to be heard."

"Thank you very much," said Gran, fumbling for her stick. "That's just what it should sound like. Good night, then, all of you, and I wish you the best of luck in the future for the women's movement, both this evening and later in life . . . and . . . don't forget that it's important that you fight it out together . . . I mean both boys and girls . . . otherwise it'll never work."

When Mia came back from Gran's room, Lotta and Håkan were in the middle of a heated argument. Håkan had got up and was standing in front of Lotta, who was sitting on the floor, scarlet in the face.

"You're just bloody snobs, the lot of you," he shouted. "Just talking a lot of crap about education and careers and sneering at housewives sitting at home gossiping and drinking coffee."

"I never said that—"

"But that's what you mean ... that women have been sloppy not to have seen to getting higher wages and status and God knows what else. You should see my mom, who's worked like mad as a cleaner all her life, early in the mornings and late at nights, so that Dad could be at home with us kids when she was out. And cleaning jobs are the only ones you can get at times like that, then you have to take the pay you're offered. Because you *need the money!* It's as simple as that. All the talk about pride in profession —who the bloody hell can afford that? Yes, your mother, sitting there with her academic qualifications and high salary ... it's simple for her to scream about education and promotion for Christ's sake—"

"Calm down, Håkan—"

"And then Mia goes and says I want a wife who'll bake cakes and mend my underpants, so that I sound as if I'm some damned old fuddy-duddy. What I want is a wife who can stay at home with my children and doesn't *have* to go out and work herself to death at some shitty job!"

"But Håkan, Håkan, calm down a bit—you've got it all wrong. I know perfectly well how you feel. But we want to *change* that now. We want all girls to get themselves training so that they can compete for better-paid jobs, and there'll be good day nurseries to put the kids in so that mothers don't have to work late at nights or early in the mornings. Don't you see, if women stick together and demand decent wages, then the men will also have to seek what you call shitty jobs. We have to learn to raise our voices, you must see, and not just go round being patient and silent—"

"But what if you don't have the energy for anything else?" snapped Håkan. "Anyway, day-care centers—a hell of lot of crap's talked about day-care centers. My older sister rushes off with her two kids to the day-care center at seven o'clock every morning and picks them up every evening, dead tired and irritable. Who says it's so darned good for kids to be in a day-care center all day, eh?"

"Who says it's so darned good for kids to hang around the heels of a nagging mom all day, then?" snapped Lotta.

"Stop!" shouted Ulla. "You must stop quarreling now, or we'll never get anywhere. The rest of us want to say something, too. For instance, I have a marvelous ad here. Here you are . . . have you seen it? A soulful guy from Hermods Correspondence College, with spectacles and a book, and then a naked girl in the background. And then the text: *I am studying through Hermods and no one but myself* [hum] *decides when and where.*"

"Dear old Hermods. Dad took his math courses through them. Usch!"

"And here," said Lena. "From the Job Center, with a lovely dame sitting rolling her eyes up to heaven and sighing into a bubble: *Professions are the same as boy-friends—at first you think there's only one in the whole world . . . then that comes to an end . . . and then you discover that there are more professions, and boyfriends, than you'd dared dream of!*"

"Those ad-agency boys must be damned empty-headed."

"And have awfully little imagination, otherwise they wouldn't keep putting naked women everywhere."

"If I were in power in this country, I'd ban all those disgusting porno pictures . . . with girls all spread out like meat on a dish," muttered Ulla.

"Oh, well, if the girls didn't pose for them, there wouldn't be any porno pictures," said Håkan curtly. "Anyway, it's not just the girls who get exploited. Guys are forced into some kind of super-sex ideal, too."

"Yes, I've got an article here which says that it's difficult to be a boy, too," said Lena. "More delicate in health, develops later, gets more depressed in puberty, it says here. And later on in life, it's mostly men who fall by the wayside—become alcoholics and criminals and so on. And at the same time, everyone expects them to be strong and brave and never to cry or show that they are afraid."

"I cry sometimes," said Per. "And I'm not especially brave."

"Yes, but," said Mia eagerly, "that's why it's so important that our roles are getting closer to each other. It's not that girls should be like boys. Girls haven't just been oppressed, for God's sake—think what a good time we've had—we don't have to go to war or hunt lions and all that. We've been allowed to sit at home and have a cozy time with our children."

"Exactly," said Per, tossing his hair back off his face. "Exactly—I'm damned well not going to be the kind of father who hardly ever sees his children . . . who's just some poor overworked breadwinner staggering home at night, and hardly that. I've seen enough of that at home. No, I think the only way would be if there was a six-hour day for *everyone*, so that both men and women could work at jobs and at home, and in politics just as much . . ."

"That sounds all right," said Lotta. "But before we get that far, women must be regarded as an equal work force with men and get equal pay and so on . . . and we'll *never* get that if we don't make the effort ourselves. Talk about quotas and all that is just crap, I think. Whatever you say, Håkan—education and unity first, then self-reliance and equal pay will come by themselves."

"I'd like a beer," said Mia.

"Gosh, it's great to be able to relax like this," mumbled Lena, creeping into the corner of the sofa with her can of beer. "Great sandwiches, Mia. I'm full . . . if I don't look out, I'll fall asleep, what with all this dim lighting and soft background music."

Lotta and Per were sitting on the floor, plucking at their guitars . . . a bit of the Beatles, a bit of Taube, a bit of Hoola Bandoola. Håkan was half lying on the sofa with his head on Ulla's lap. Mia was lolling over the arm of Gran's armchair, keeping a sleepy hostess eye on the beer and the sandwich plate.

"Don't any of you really want another sandwich?"

"Did you hear that the Eight is going to take us to *The Love Show* at the Klara Theatre? . . . It's about sex roles, you know?"

"Goody."

"Have we finished this . . . I mean, do we have to go on talking about it this evening?" said Håkan, slowly running his hand down Ulla's leg.

"Finished? You're nuts. We've lots more to do."

"But the Eight said it shouldn't be too long."

"I've found a lovely poem," said Mia. "Quiet, now. Don't munch so, Håkan.

> *"You sought a flower*
> *and found a fruit*
> *You sought a well*
> *and found an ocean*
> *You sought a woman—*
> *and found a soul*
> *You are disappointed."*

"Who wrote that?" mumbled Per.

"Who was it now? Yes, she's a Finnish author . . . Söder . . . Södergren, no Södergran. Isn't it good?"

"I wonder if it's true," said Per, looking up at Mia. "I mean that bit about disappointment."

"Gustaf, have I got any clean blouses?" Lotta called out suddenly.

"Why shouldn't a woman help with the washing up as a matter of course?" asked Lena.

"My husband is not going to have to go to work, not while the children are small," Ulla filled in.

"Men have no sense of humor," Mia said, sighing.

"What the hell is all that?" said Håkan irritably, propping himself up on his elbow.

They all burst out laughing. "Didn't you notice . . . they're all those male clichés the other way around?"

"Uh . . ."

"We haven't discussed solidarity," said Ulla suddenly, sitting up. "All that about female jealousy and that we speak ill of each other. Because it's true, isn't it?"

"But that's because women have always been an oppressed group, who've been forced to compete for men's favors." Lotta put down her guitar and intoned in mild preaching tones, "Oppressed groups have no solidarity with their own group. They can't *afford* to. Remember that there have always been more women than men, and it was a matter of fastening onto a man to be supported . . . and anyway, who invented all those nasty stories about female jealousy—men, of course—they fit in excellently."

"Don't men slander each other, then?" asked Ulla.

"Yes, but then it's called *factual criticism* and not gossip," said Lotta, snorting.

"Oh, heavens, is it really that late?" said Ulla, sighing and holding her wrist watch up to a flickering candle. "I don't think we've made much headway at all . . . There's so much to discuss, it makes your head spin."

"We must go home now . . ."

"I'll just read one more thing," said Lena. "A clipping from a paper—it's called 'Women's Liberation Means Love to Men.'"

"Okay . . . it sounds all right."

"How can women's struggle for liberation mean love to men, when we continually urge women to rebel against men and accuse them of oppression?" Lena read rather hesitantly in the candlelight. "I won't read it all . . . *The oppressor does not always need to use force—it is sufficient that he always gives himself precedence . . . Men dominate women in our society. What a man does and says is valued most, not because he is malicious but because he has been exposed to indoctrination in his male role, which makes him into the oppressor. It is the oppressor in men*

that we are attacking. The important thing is that we don't give in, whether for the sake of domestic peace or for the sake of our love . . .

"Our resistance to men is an explanation of our program. We explain that we want to include him with us in the work of building up a society in which no one dominates over others . . . women's struggle for liberation is love of human beings. All human beings."

"Amen," said Håkan, kissing Ulla's ear.

"We can use that as a conclusion . . . it's great . . . and just what your grandmother said, too," said Per. "That we have to work on this together. I think all this quarreling with each other is so feeble in some way."

"But we have to make a *fuss*, otherwise nothing happens at all, don't you see?" said Lotta. "But now we really must go home."

After the "sex roles gang," with a great deal of giggling and tiptoeing and suppressed noise, had finally removed themselves from Mia's hall and got into the elevator, Mia noticed that the light was still on in Gran's room. Anxiously she opened the door a little.

"Are you all right? Did we disturb you? We went on much longer than I thought we would."

"No . . . you didn't disturb me. You've been as quiet as mice this last hour or so. It was a pity I didn't have the energy for more . . . it was really an experience meeting your friends. They're so open and natural and nice."

"Yes, they really *are* nice. And it's great doing a group project like this—you're sort of welded together in a special way—even if you do have different views."

"Yes, it must be very good for you to be made to go into a subject a bit more thoroughly like that."

"Yes, it is, I think," said Mia slowly, sitting down on the rug by the bed. "This all seems to me . . . very important, in some way. I seem to have found out things that I've never thought about before. It's funny, isn't it, that you don't seem to grasp what is happening around you properly."

"Haven't you ever been interested in politics?"

"Not really. To be honest, I've been somewhat put off by all that stuff Dad is mixed up in . . . it always seemed so deadly dull. But that's wrong, of course."

"I think I thought like that when I was young," said Gran, "until I found out that politics wasn't some dreary independent force, but that—well, that politics is in fact everything . . . everything that affects us."

Mia sat in silence, feeling satisfied with the evening, her anxiety and uncertainty dissolved. She leaned forward and stroked Gran's hand, which was hanging over the edge of the bed. The swollen blue veins felt like soft ridges beneath her fingers.

"I like you so much, Gran," she said, pressing her forehead against the edge of the bed so that Gran could not see her eyes.

"Me, too, Mia love," said Gran, and Mia heard her voice thickening a little. She was silent for a moment and then went on, "I feel a bit like Simeon in the temple."

"What did he do?"

"It was he who said when he had seen Jesus, 'Lord, now lettest thou thy servant depart in peace.' "

"Don't you dare!"

Mia stayed sitting on the rug, enjoying the silence. The nursery wallpaper's colored birds and flowers were like a warm decorative bower. Lillan's old drawings and pictures of horses were still on the walls. The blind wasn't pulled down, as Gran liked being wakened by the first morning light. Outside the window lay a broad cotton-wool layer of fresh snow, not yet melted. The room smelled good, of Gran's eau de cologne mixed with the slight smell of medicine. The clock on the bedside table was ticking away quietly and evenly, as soporific as a buzzing insect. Mia closed her eyes, feeling voluptuously tired rather than sleepy. And full of love.

Suddenly she heard from a change in Gran's breathing that she was asleep. Slowly she withdrew her hand and turned off the light.

She crept out through the door on tiptoe.

$\mathcal{M}$IA woke up slowly and carefully, with her eyes closed, fumbling for the pillow and not finding it, opening her eyes and staring at strange wallpaper, yellow roses on a beige background, staring without understanding.

She rolled over on to her back, as heavy as a sack. Stale cigarette smoke stung her nostrils, and there was a horrible sour taste in her mouth. When she ran her tongue over her teeth, they were rough and furred, and it was difficult to swallow.

The sun was throwing shadowy stripes from the slats of

the Venetian blind, and the white Japanese paper lamp-shade swam like a ship's buoy above her head. She turned her eyes without moving her body—Beethoven glaring at her with a frown from the wall opposite, an empty wine glass standing on the dressing table, and her new dress in a heap on a chair.

Mia lay still, trying to remember.

Her head was throbbing slightly, and it hurt when she moved her legs.

She was lying in someone's white painted double bed, beneath a striped green quilt, underneath which she was naked, her body warm and soft with sleep. The space beside her was empty, but his yellow-and-blue pants were hanging on the bedpost.

She closed her eyes again.

She had drunk too much red wine. She didn't know that she tolerated so little red wine, or perhaps it wasn't all that little?

And now she was lying in Martin's sister and brother-in-law's double bed in a fifth-floor apartment in Hallonbergen. She had no idea what the time was; her watch had stopped at three o'clock.

They had been celebrating Martin's twenty-first birthday.

Martin had called the previous week and asked if she wanted to come to his birthday party—he had been lent his sister's apartment and there was to be quite a crowd. Bosse and Anna, of course, and Lena.

There didn't seem to be any question of refusing or not. It was decided the moment Martin had spoken her name.

"Mia?"

"Yes."

They had all drunk too much. They danced and sang and made speeches. It was a wonderful party . . .

They sang a great deal—everything, old children's songs, Beatles songs, Dylan, Bellman, top of the pops . . . and Martin played for them.

Then people grew tired, sat down on sofas and chairs and on the floor and kissed and cuddled. Bosse and Anna vanished into the other room. Lena went to make coffee in the kitchen with Joakim. Mia didn't notice when they left the apartment. Strange, because it had been arranged that she would spend the night with Lena and Bosse, so that she didn't wake up Gran and Dad so late at night.

It was unreal in some way; she had never felt like this with Jan. The first times had been the most difficult. It had been disappointing. Anyway, it had never been especially good with Jan. He came so quickly that she could never keep up. She had pretended, just to keep him happy the the last time.

This was different. Perhaps he had had a lot of girls. It was funny that she didn't mind any longer. That was the wine, perhaps, the excitement and the inhibitions that had vanished. He had been so sweet, trying to adjust to her. It wasn't his fault that it hadn't been perfect. But it had been enough that she could now understand what it was all about . . . all she'd read about . . . that Lena had told her about . . . something like explosions of ecstasy and desire. She had only touched on it, but that was enough.

But where had Martin gone?

She had thought he was in the bathroom.

It ought to feel horrible to wake up like this, alone in a stranger's bed . . . almost like a . . . like a . . .

The front door clicked. Mia sat up in terror . . . God, supposing it was Martin's sister and brother-in-law coming back home? But then she calmed down—they had gone to the country, for heaven's sake.

As she sat up, she felt how much her head was aching and how swollen and tender she was. Suddenly it was terribly unpleasant to be lying there like somebody's rag doll in an unknown person's bed.

"Would you care for a little early-morning coffee, Madame Mia?"

Martin propped open the door with the tray and stood there in the doorway, unashamedly bright and fresh. He was wearing nothing but a trench coat over his jeans.

"Good morning, my beauty—did you sleep well?"

"What . . . have you been *out*? There's a smell of fresh pastries."

"Yes, we have an excellent little store in the next building which opens on Sundays. Here you are." He put the tray down on the bed.

"Oh, that looks good . . ."

There was a rose lying by her cup. Two large glasses of ice-cold juice. Four pastries on a blue glass plate . . . the smell of vanilla blended deliciously with the smell of coffee.

In a glass was a toothbrush in a sealed plastic cover.

"And a *toothbrush* . . . you're crazy, so fantastic . . . a toothbrush. You *are* sweet."

"Yes, I thought it'd taste good."

"Just a moment." Mia snatched up the toothbrush and vanished into the bathroom. A few minutes later she came back, her hair brushed and combed and her face washed.

"I stole a little of your toothpaste and a drop of Femme from a bottle, only a little drop. Oh, juice is just what I need. My throat's as dry as sandpaper."

Martin had pulled up the blind and the sun was streaming in onto the yellow rug and glinting on the thermos of coffee. A transistor radio that Martin had brought in from the kitchen was broadcasting some Sunday-morning Mozart.

When they had finished, they both lay back, smoking cigarettes, Martin laughing at Mia's clumsy efforts, as she didn't usually smoke.

"It feels great," she said contentedly, blowing smoke into his face. "Like in a French film."

He laughed.

"You were great last night," he said, putting his free arm round her naked shoulders.

"I drank too much," said Mia.

"Do you need an excuse?"

"We—ell, perhaps not." She said nothing for a moment. "But in some way, it seems disgusting to go to bed with someone just because you're a little tight."

"You mean you wouldn't have done it otherwise?" Martin stroked her gently on the throat. "Do you really mean that?"

"I don't know."

Martin stubbed his cigarette out in the saucer and bent over her.

"But now you're not tight any longer, are you, my darling? Then I'll show you how fine it can be, even when you're as sober as a judge."

"Now?" Mia mumbled, half suffocated under his kiss.

· 88 ·

But his hand was already on its way down her breast and stomach, and she shivered with pleasure.

"Yes, right now," muttered Martin. "It's never so good as on the morning after the night before. You're rested and warm and you've got the whole day in front of you."

"You're crazy," she whispered, putting her arm round his neck. "Was that why you bought a toothbrush for me?"

"Not just because of that."

A long time later Mia called up Lena. It turned out that Lena had already called up Mia's father and said that Mia would be back late.

Mia giggled. "You might say that, certainly."

"And so I said that we would probably go for a walk in Haga Park as the weather was so fine."

"Shall we?"

"Yes, if you want to. We're sitting here waiting with ham and eggs."

"Great! We're starving . . . aren't we, Martin?"

"Aha," said Lena.

"And what did Dad say about my not coming home all day?"

"He said it was a marvelous idea. You'd need the fresh air, he said, after the night's exercise."

"What . . . did he say exercise?"

"No, but that's what I say."

"When shall we meet again?" said Mia as they kissed good-bye in Mia's elevator that afternoon. By pressing the button up and down to and from the seventh floor, they managed to fit in quite a number of kisses. "No, now we must stop," said Mia, panting. "People are banging on the elevator doors down there. When shall we meet again?"

Martin frowned. "I've got an awful lot of tests this week, but I'll call as soon as I can."

It was Thursday evening, nearly nine o'clock. Gran had gone to bed, and Dad was sitting in front of the television waiting for the news. Mia was lying on her bed, grinding away at English grammar with a bag of raspberry jelly beans. She had just decided to resign herself as far as Thursday was concerned.

It was idiotic. Insanely foolish.

Going around like any other silly idiot, waiting for the phone to ring, asking carefully if by any chance anyone had called. She knew he had a lot of tests, didn't she? He'd said so.

But he could have *called* all the same. They could just listen to each other's voice—say hello, how are you, thanks for the party, your rose is still alive, talk a little, ask what was going on.

It didn't take all that time to dial a number.

Why didn't she do it herself then? What kind of damned equality was this?

We can take the initiative if we want contact with a man —that's what it had said in that book on sisterhood—*we can ask someone to dance with us, call and suggest a meeting and we can offer sexual invitations*—ha ha, that was easy for those old girls to say.

Anyway, she had in fact called once. But no one had answered.

She had called Lena, too.

Lena was all right. Joakim was doing his national service

and had gone back to Norrtälje on Sunday evening. That was all right because then you knew where you were with each other. And anyway, Joakim called every evening.

"What are you doing otherwise?" said Lena.

"Learning irregular verbs . . . what are you doing?"

"Reading about an interview with Onassis' maid."

"*Who* did you say?"

"Onassis' maid. You've no idea what fascinating things she reveals about Jackie and Onassis! And then I'm going to wallow in how Eva Aulin sacrifices all for love and about Barbra Streisand's stormy love life."

"Sounds nice, lying there like a sponge. Though you ought to be ashamed of yourself—what would the Eight say?"

"I am ashamed," said Lena cheerfully. "But when you've got a cold and a thick head like I have, then it's trash like that you need."

"What about Anna's party on Saturday?"

"It'll have to be put off, I'm afraid. She's in bed with a temperature, poor girl. It must have been a bit too early to celebrate the spring in Haga Park last Sunday."

"Was Martin going to it?"

"I don't know—haven't you spoken to him?"

"He's got a whole lot of tests this week."

Hell, how thirsty raspberry jelly beans made you.

"Telephone for you," said Dad, poking his head around the door.

"For me? Who is it?" Mia got up so quickly that her English grammar flew across the floor.

Dad smiled. "Some youth."

"Hello." Mia tried to stop her voice from sounding too happy.

"Hi, this is Martin . . . what are you up to?"

"I'm doing English grammar."

"God, how awful. What about coming to the movies?"

"Now? It's past nine, isn't it?"

"Ten to . . . if you hustle a bit, we'd make it to the Cosmorama. They're showing *The Sting.*"

When Mia came tumbling out with her coat still undone, Martin was standing there waiting beside an old Volvo.

"I've borrowed this old crate from a friend for a few days," he said.

"But we don't need a car to go to the Cosmorama."

"I wasn't thinking of going to the movies, either," said Martin, pulling her to him and kissing her hard.

"Why did you say so then?" said Mia, pushing him away.

"Are you really dying to see *The Sting* then?"

"But why did you say so?"

"Darling," Martin laughed, opening the car door—"I'll give you three guesses."

"You're mad." Mia let herself be guided into the car without offering any resistance. "You're crazy."

"That's just what I am," said Martin contentedly, starting the engine. "Wise and beautiful and in the prime of life, as they say."

Mia laughed and put her head down on his shoulder. "But I have to be home by eleven at the latest, because I've got an English test tomorrow."

"As you like, madame," said Martin, blowing out his long mustache. "We can get a lot done in two hours."

Mia had never been to Martin's place before. The room was dominated by a wide bed and a piano. On the walls hung a guitar, a lute, and a great many concert posters. Piles of sheet music and books lay neatly stacked on chairs and the table, and an open clarinet case lay on the floor. The bed was made and the ashtrays empty.

"What a nice room," said Mia. "And how neat it is."

"Yes, old Sis has been here and cleaned up today, otherwise it's usually pretty grubby."

"What? Do you mean to say your sister comes and cleans for you . . . that's the absolute limit. For God's sake, surely you could do that yourself?"

"Maybe. But it was Mom who fixed all that up . . . so that dear little Martin shouldn't die in squalor." Martin laughed mirthlessly and sat down at the piano. "Come and kiss me and don't look so damned women's lib . . . it doesn't suit you."

Martin was lying on his stomach, asleep. His long hair fell over his face, and he looked like a little boy, despite his mustache. His breathing was light and even; now and again he sighed in his sleep, one arm flung across Mia.

The lamp Martin had put on the floor gave the room a mysterious reddish light, like a cave. Mia found herself filled with tenderness.

I love him, she thought. I have never been so happy as I am with him. With her free hand, she stroked his cheek, and he peered up at her through his eyelashes and smiled.

"Do you like me?" she said.

"Of course I like you, otherwise I wouldn't sleep with you," he mumbled sleepily, nibbling at her fingers.

Mia withdrew her hand. Martin opened his eyes wide. "Wasn't it good? I thought you came—"

"Oh, yes."

"Then let's sleep a bit longer, shall we . . . ?"

It was Saturday afternoon, an icy March Saturday, white light ruthlessly pouring through the window, revealing how pale and wan she was looking. Mia was standing in front of the big mirror in the living room, looking at the dark circles under her eyes.

She was alone at home.

Gran had her doctor's permission to go to the Workers Educational Association centenary dinner, to which she had been invited in her capacity as Grandad's wife. She had begged and begged and finally the doctor had given in. Dad was escorting her. They had just left in a taxi, Gran in her cherry-red dress, her pearl earrings, and with her embroidered silk handbag.

Mia wasn't really standing in front of the mirror to examine her appearance. She had just stopped there during her wanderings around the apartment.

It was pleasant walking around an empty apartment . . . from room to room, trying to get your thoughts in order, feeling that lump in your stomach.

Lately she seemed to have been living on several different levels, as if afflicted by a division of her personality, not just into two but into several Mias with different problems. Like those Russian painted wooden dolls that Granny had on her chest of drawers.

It was confusing and exhausting.

Deep down inside her, clamped down and constricted,

was the Mia who was in love with Martin, the one who went around waiting for telephone calls. There was nothing much she could do about that at the moment; it was nothing to talk about, not even with Lena. Nothing to do but wait and hope and keep from crying at night; because he hadn't got in touch again; because a strange girl had answered the telephone when Mia had taken her courage into her own hands and phoned the week before.

The Mia coping with school really had the best time of it.

The group project on sex roles was a great success. There was a violent and marvelous argument in the class after the group presented its material, and the Eight was very pleased. That evening they went to *The Love Show* and afterward Lotta's mother invited them back to tea and sandwiches.

Even her English test went quite well, oddly enough.

Perhaps she should wash her hair. . . . It looked awful, and she always thought so well under the drier. Gran had given her one of those real ones with a cap, for her birthday, so that she wouldn't run about and catch cold with her long wet hair.

The most difficult level at the moment was the family.

It was this stupid Easter holiday that was causing all the trouble. Mother had called again this morning.

She wanted to know what was going to happen. She couldn't understand why they couldn't make up their minds about who was going to see whom.

God, what a tangle.

Mia turned on the record player and took out the end record on the shelf. It happened to be "Pinewood Rally."

She turned up the volume. That was good, sitting shut in inside the wall of thunderous sound.

Then a cheese sandwich, and a Coke, and the rest of the box of chocolates Mother had sent.

Oh, Mother, Mother, how difficult everything is. Oh, if only she were a little older, if only she were in her last term at school. Jesus, what a long time it took to grow up when you went to school for so long. It seemed such a hopelessly long time to go still, and yet time went by so quickly, in one way . . .

That an Easter holiday could cause so much silly fuss and bother.

Dad was longing to see Lillan. Mother was longing to see Mia. Mia, of course, was also longing for Mother, and for Lillan. But at the same time she didn't want to leave Gran, and on top of that she didn't want to leave town because of Martin. In case.

But she couldn't tell Mother that, and if Martin had another girl, then . . .

Then it was also clear that Dad missed Mother a lot, and that she clearly had no particular wish to see him at the moment.

A crazy mess, the whole thing.

Mother had sounded tired and cross on the phone. Lillan had had chickenpox and Granny had flu.

In the middle of it all, a letter had come from Jan this morning to say that he was coming back from Matfors after Easter and that he was ashamed he had been such a bad letter writer and he hoped they would meet again. There was a lot he understood better now, he wrote.

I'll go mad, thought Mia.

Deep down, she knew that everything was much more complicated than that. That it wasn't just the Easter holiday and who should go and see whom. It was the future coming nearer, the divorce, the decision, when the trial period was over, and all that would come with it.

This business of Gran . . . whether she'd manage.

This business with the apartment, which had become too large and expensive.

This business of being separated permanently . . . forever . . . drifting apart, becoming more and more alien.

God, if only she could run away from it all, far, far away, where there were no longings or feelings or decisions or responsibility, where you could put your head in the sand and say to hell with it all.

Just as Mia turned off the drier, the telephone rang. She was so surprised the words almost stuck in her throat.

"Oh, yes, hi . . . hi . . ."

"I'm in the pub down here . . . do you feel like coming down for a while, if you've nothing better to do?"

"Well, I must stay at home and wait for Gran. She's at a dinner, but she has to leave early."

"What do you mean . . . is the old girl out on the town? You mean to say you're *alone* at home? Then I'll come up for a while for a chat, if I may. . . ."

"Do that . . ."

"Bye for now, then. I'll buy something at The Corner, and then you'll make some tea, won't you?"

As Mia brushed her hair like lightning and threw a clean blouse on, she felt a new decisiveness growing within her. She'd show him, indeed she would. Damned pasha.

He was not going to be allowed to lord it over her any

old way . . . crooking his little finger, come hither, kiss me, sleep with me . . .

What was she herself doing? She was brushing her hair and making herself beautiful . . . what was she after? The same as he was. She wanted to, she too . . .

Though she wanted it to be something more.

Suddenly he was there, standing in the hall with a bag of buns and two yellow crocuses he had swiped from the caretaker's flowerbed.

"Long time no see," he said boisterously, taking her in his arms, kissing her hard and putting the crocuses in her hair.

"What a great apartment you've got here," said Martin, going over to the window in the living room. "Look, you can see almost right over to Hallonbergen from here. And there's that old Datema star sitting there staring . . . did you know that Joakim works there?"

"No, I didn't know that," mumbled Mia, trying to twist herself away from his grasp around her waist.

"What a terrific blouse, darling . . . is it new?" He put his hand on her breast. "Do you know, madame, that you're a real knockout?"

"The kettle's boiling," said Mia, removing his hands. "Then I want to talk to you."

"*Talk?*" he said, looking comically dismayed.

After they'd had tea and eaten The Corner's delicious currant buns, Mia pushed away her cup and sat back in the corner of the sofa. Martin stretched out his hand to pull her to him.

"For God's sake, Mia, why are we wasting our time talking?" he said with a grimace.

"Do you realize that I've been in hell for the last few weeks, Martin? Sitting at home here waiting like a well-behaved sheep for you to phone . . . for you graciously to raise your little finger and call me to you . . . for you graciously to make me happy . . . ?"

"Oh, hell, Mia, what *are* you talking about? I never promised anything, did I? You knew what I was like, for Christ's sake."

"What do you mean? Did I know?"

"But we're modern, free people, for Christ's sake, we don't live in the days of our parents, when you couldn't jump into bed without first going to a priest."

"Who may I ask is talking about a priest?"

"I mean . . . shouldn't one be allowed to have some fun together for a night or two without being hung on the hook for ever? Why do girls always bring in emotions and crap like that? Isn't it damned nice that we've got over that puritanism and romanticism and love with a capital L . . . that the pill and that kind of thing has given us a blasted good freedom?"

"Don't you see that that freedom isn't just for *men*?" cried Mia. "That it's a blasted fine freedom for you, I can quite believe. You, who just go around picking out girls and giving them perfect orgasms, like a kind of super–sex machine in which the main thing is that you feel as little as possible to succeed as much as possible."

"And you, who're always talking about sex roles and women's lib," interrupted Martin angrily, catching hold of Mia's wrist. "You modern liberated girls pretend that you want equality with boys in all fields and when you at last get it in sex, then you dredge up that same old romantic-love morality which you've used for a hundred years! You've damned well got to decide which way you want it to be."

"I'm not talking about romantic-love morality. I'm talking about feelings. I don't want to be a sex machine, with perfect technique and super-great proficiency."

"What's wrong with that? What's wrong with being good in bed, may I ask?"

"So you mean that sex is to be isolated from people's emotional life? What's wrong with liking the man you're sleeping with and whom you want to be together with in other ways too, talking, getting to know each other, understanding . . ."

"The one doesn't exclude the other, for Christ's sake! Of course a girl can say no if she doesn't want to and yes if she does. The main thing is surely that you know where you are with each other?"

"Do all your girls know where they are with you from the beginning? Was it only *me* who was such an absolute idiot that I thought I had something more to offer than just bed? To think that I fell for that stuff with the rose and the toothbrush—crash! I presume your bathroom cupboard is jam-packed with used-only-once toothbrushes! Dear sweet little Martin, indeed . . ."

"Must you spoil that lovely morning we had in the sun . . . which was so great?" said Martin, getting to his feet.

"You're the one who's spoiled it," said Mia thickly.

Martin went over to the window and stood there silently for a while, his back to Mia. Then he turned quickly around, went over to her, and took hold of her by the shoulders.

"Mia . . . I'm sorry . . . I'm sorry if I hurt you. I know I'm a damned egoist."

He smiled pleadingly with all his white teeth, his soft hair, redolent of shampoo, hanging down and tickling her cheek.

"There's nothing really to be sorry about," mumbled Mia. "I have only myself to blame."

Martin dropped his hands and went over and sat down at the other end of the sofa. He took out a pack of cigarettes and shook a cigarette half out, then changed his mind and put it back again. Mia saw that he was sitting with his head in his hands.

Neither of them said anything. Mia heard the church clock striking seven.

"Do you have another girl now?"

"What do you mean—*do I have*?"

"I mean . . . are you together with another girl aside from me?"

"I thought you'd caught on how I felt about it. That I think it's great being with girls . . . having a good time together . . . good in bed together. But you talk of being together as if it meant owning each other in some way . . . as if sex were something shady you have to dress up in a whole lot of feelings and promises and things."

"So you're afraid then?"

"What do you mean, afraid?"

"I mean afraid of feelings . . . of something that'll disturb your fine free sex-machine life?"

"Okay . . . of course one wants to be free—one doesn't want to tie oneself down."

"Tie oneself down? You sound as if all girls wanted to drag you off to the priest, or whatever it is nowadays. You don't understand a single thing about what I'm talking about. Girls aren't all that eager to tie themselves down, either . . . to be stuck in Tensta or somewhere with a husband and children." She fell silent for a while, creeping farther up into the sofa, her legs curled under her.

"I'm talking about feelings . . . of gettting something more from each other than just that moment when you're in bed. You've had lots of girls . . . have you never been in love?"

"In love . . . what is *in love*? Of course I've liked lots of them—you, for instance, Mia—listen . . ." Martin turned to her and smiled, not his great seducer's grin, but almost with embarrassment. "Mia, wasn't it good together for us? That Sunday was great, wasn't it? All day, like a kind of happiness, when we scuttled about in Haga Park and laughed and messed about and were crazy? Those were feelings, too, for God's sake, weren't they? Damned good feelings."

"Yes, yes," said Mia gently. "That's just why I want them to last a little longer than a day."

Martin said nothing.

Mia suddenly laughed. "Martin, you look just like a little boy who's dropped his ice cream."

Relieved to hear her laugh, he got up quickly, grinning cheerfully. "Mia," he said, bending over her and stroking her cheek with the back of his hand. "Mia . . . you're not angry with me, are you?"

Mia went on laughing. It wasn't *worth* . . .

"Then we're friends, are we?" He moved closer.

"Friends? I thought that's *just* what we *weren't*! I thought I was nothing but your ex-mattress."

"*Mia!*"

"No, leave me alone . . ."

"Mia, now that we know where we are with each other, so to speak, can't we . . don't you want to? To show that you're not angry with me?"

He got down on his knees beside her and began stroking her breast with gentle hands.

"You're hopeless, Martin . . . you great idiot. You're absolutely hopeless!" Mia leaned over with a laugh and kissed the tip of his nose. "But you're sweet. Though you haven't a clue about anything."

"I certainly have," he said, beginning to fumble with the buttons of her blouse.

"No, Martin," murmured Mia, making a feeble attempt to push his hands away.

"Yes, let's meet as those dreadful sex machines you keep talking about. Mia, darling . . . I can feel that you want to, too."

They rolled down onto the rug. "Help, there goes my zipper!"

"Oh, God . . ."

"What now?"

"Wait, I'll be back." She kissed him on the nose and vanished into the bathroom.

The clock struck eight times tinnily and Mia just heard it beyond his kisses.

"It sounds a bit moralistic today," she murmured.

"What the hell are you talking about?"

"The church clock," she giggled.

"Church clocks are supposed to sound moralistic, for God's sake."

Mia stood by the kitchen window and watched Martin's light trench coat disappearing through the dark bushes down in the yard.

She was feeling strangely free and light of heart.

And yet nothing had really changed. She was still there with her romantic love. She didn't know if she would ever be with Martin again. Or who knows . . .

But she had learned a little, seen through a little of this business of living.

$\mathcal{J}$T was almost ten on Sunday morning when Dad came in with the coffee tray.

"Heavens, is it that late? It's still dark almost," said Mia, sitting up in confusion.

"Yes, it's raining, the heavy spring rains . . . The clouds are right down to the roofs," said Dad, letting up the blind. "I haven't seen so much rain since the fall."

"How are things with Gran today?" Mia asked, biting into her toast and marmalade. "Is she very tired after the party?"

"Yes. She says she'll probably stay in bed today. I think she had a bit of pain in the night But otherwise she's enormously pleased."

"Isn't it great that it went so well and that so many people she'd known were there. She seemed quite exhilarated last night."

"Yes, and it was great fun for me, too. There were so many people there I haven't seen for ages. It was fun seeing how respected Mom was. I didn't have the slightest idea she'd been so active in her day."

"It seems in fact that you knew very little about . . . I mean . . . it seems to be difficult to keep in contact with your parents when you grow up."

"You're right there . . . that's true. There've been a lot of . . . a lot of empty years between us." He was sitting in the rocking chair, rocking slowly as he spoke. "That's why I'm so grateful to you, Mia-Pia, for arranging for Mom to come here." He fell silent again, then went on, "It's not just that at last I think I've got to know a little about her and . . . about Father. I've also learned a lot about myself. Lots of things have been explained. It's strange that it should be so difficult to talk to each other . . . about important things." He fell silent again and lit his pipe, which had gone out. "I never seemed to . . . when I was growing up. Father was so dominating with all his kindness and Mom worshiped him. And then all my brothers and sisters, who always seemed to be in the way"—he laughed—"I thought."

"No," he went on, "this won't do. I must be off soon. You haven't forgotten that I'm off to a conference in Sigtuna and won't be back until tomorrow afternoon? Rune Axelson is picking me up in his car in a minute."

"Don't worry. I'll look after the household," said Mia, thrusting her legs out of the bed. "We'll have a lovely cozy women's day, Gran and I, talking and everything . . . so you just go and have a nice time with all those old gents of yours."

"There'll be at least as many women as men there," said Dad, laughing.

"So much the better."

"What a welcome and perfect rainy day," said Mia contentedly, sinking into Gran's armchair. "Usually one's furious when it rains on Sunday in the spring."

"I must say you look like a newly washed spring day, too, my girl," said Gran, examining Mia's face. "Indeed, you look happy for the first time in several weeks."

"Does it show . . . so much?" said Mia, flushing slightly and laughing.

Gran smiled.

"I don't really know why I feel so happy today," Mia went on. "I'm really just as unhappily in love, or whatever you call it, as I was yesterday. But I had . . . a kind of reckoning with Martin yesterday, and with myself, actually. We cleared up certain notions. And that feels good. But tell me more about yesterday—who you met and so on. I heard so little last night."

"Well, it really was a splendid evening," said Gran, her pale face lighting up. "It was as if Gustaf were alive again. Everyone spoke so highly of him, and of his parents. And it all came back to me again, all that time when we were young and energetic and wanted to do things. It was great fun that Arne was with me, too, and could hear all about that time. He has never belonged to the WEA—has never understood what it meant then. It was so gay—banners and flowers and fine speeches and greetings. Well, I made myself stay longer than the doctor allowed, but I didn't want to leave in the middle of the meal, especially as I had such a nice gentleman beside me—his father had been a colleague of Gustaf's. He remembered everything about him. He was so tall and handsome, people always remember him."

"You look so proud, as if you'd just fallen in love, when

you talk about Grandad," said Mia, teasingly. "You're almost blushing. It must be great to sound like that when you're seventy."

"It's not fashionable nowadays to stick together with the same person all your life."

"All marriages weren't happy in your day, either, were they?"

"No, good heavens, no. That was a stupid thing to say. If you're lucky, then you're just lucky, and luck you can have any time."

Mia sat silently looking out of the window, where the rain was still streaming down the panes. She shivered slightly and drew Gran's white woolly shawl more tightly around her shoulders.

"Gran," she said hesitantly. "Do you think . . . do you think Mother and Dad will get a divorce? Do you think all that talk about a trial period was just pretending—that actually they had already decided last fall?"

"I don't know, Mia. Marianne had perhaps already decided, but Arne hasn't, as far as I can make out."

"No, actually, I think he misses Mother terribly . . . it seems so. But she doesn't want to come up and see him, though she could stay with Aunt Vera."

"Yes, you heard that I was welcome to go back to the Home?" said Gran quickly.

"Yes, but only over Easter, promise me . . . Gran, dearest. Aren't you all right here, then? It'd be awfully empty if you moved out . . . and Dad's so pleased to be with you like this. He said so only this morning."

"Thank you, dear. You know I want to . . . but we'll have to see how things go."

Gran lay back against her heap of pillows without speaking. She had taken out some boxes of old photographs, which she was sorting through into bundles, writing names on the backs.

"In a few years, when I've left home, Dad'll be so dreadfully lonely if they divorce," said Mia thoughtfully.

"Perhaps he'll find someone else?"

"Dad? Do you really think so?" said Mia doubtfully.

"It wouldn't be all that odd . . . a man in his prime needs a woman in both one way and another."

"Yes, but he's so . . . so *old* . . . I mean, quite old."

Gran laughed. "You're still so young that you think that love and sex are something you're only concerned with when you're under forty. Oh, my dear, that's a perpetual false notion among the young. No one can ever believe their parents did anything like that! I'll have you know, Mia, my love, that the last time I slept with your grandfather, he was seventy-two, and that was three years before he died."

"Gosh, I really didn't know that . . . I thought, I thought . . . that everything like that came to an end . . . at the change of life and all that."

"You don't read your advice columns in the magazines properly," said Gran, smiling. "You can learn all sorts of things from them. But young people just read about their own problems, I imagine."

After lunch Mia went into Gran's room with a bundle of clothes and her sewing bag under her arm.

"I'm going to take this opportunity to do some mending," she said, sitting down at the table by the window. "I haven't mended a thing for ages, and soon I won't have a whole seam left!"

Gran was still sorting her photographs and reading old letters. They sat in silence for a while, the only sound the monotonous dripping of the rain. Although it was only two o'clock, it was so dark that Mia had turned on the light.

"Gran," said Mia suddenly. "Isn't it really rather nice to be old and wise? Like you . . ."

"Ha, ha," mocked Gran, looking up from a picture of Grandad in his Sunday best among baby carriages outside the Copper Tent in Haga Park. "Well, old and wise— wise—what's that, may I ask? That you've had a lot of experience. But who cares about other people's experiences? Everyone wants to experience things for themselves." She fell silent. "You get a little more tolerant, yes," she went on. "But, it'd be a terrible shame if you didn't get a little more indulgent with the years, I think. You're bound to learn some understanding and see through some things. Perhaps it's just laziness, anyway . . . resignation, to use a better word. Though I don't think I'm all that resigned, indeed no. I fought against that with all my strength, be- cause it's tempting to become resigned when you've been around for a while. In this life, with its wars and hatreds and dreams of power and the Kingdom of Heaven . . . you can get tired of less."

"But Gran, you're so . . . I mean, you seem so interested in what's happening now. You don't just snort at every- thing and think everything's crazy, like Grandpa does, for instance. He thinks everything was so good before and that now the world is heading for disaster . . ."

"Well, that's probably pure chance . . . what one is like . . . and where you live, and what contacts you make at work. I really do thank my Creator that I had such a lot to do with young people in the office ... before I was ill. And it *is* difficult to take in how quickly everything changes, all the same ... that what you worked for and thought was the only right thing has suddenly gone by. And you feel you don't have the energy, that it's not really worth beginning to take an interest in anything new. It's easy to become grumpy and suspicious. I felt that in the Home—you were sort of sucked into the world of the old, the world of pains and God and cakes, in a way that was quite paralyzing. Even if you tried to read and keep up, there wasn't anyone who could be bothered to discuss it with you. No, but look, I've found that poem that I cut out the other day," she said suddenly in a different voice, holding out a clipping.

"What poem was that?"

"Well, you see," said Gran, with a slightly embarrassed laugh, "I've always been interested in those little poems you find in the death columns."

"Why?"

"Well, why ... ? I don't really know when it began. ... Perhaps it was the only poetry I ever saw as a child."

"But aren't they all more or less the same? All that about farewell and sleep well and trees that sough in the wind with melancholy and angels that smile down on you?"

"Oh, yes, most of them are just standard poems that people get from the undertaker's ... often Christmas-present rhymes. But I like them all the same. It's touching in some way that they survive in an age of computers. I used to try to work out why they chose just this or that poem, and what the person was like in real life, and that sort of thing. Then there were poems people wrote them-selves, and hymns, and the great poets."

"Perhaps it's because people want to say something kind and loving, which they weren't allowed to say when they were alive . . . or just something beautiful . . . ?"

"Perhaps. Yes, maybe. It used to be mostly Wallin, but now they're mostly Pär Lagerkvist. Though they can get outworn, too, the poets. I always used to think those lines of Erik Lindegren's—*Somewhere within us,/we are always together*—were the loveliest I knew."

"But what was it that you cut out . . . was it especially lovely?"

"It was this . . . it's old Scandinavian, I think. It's so good, you'd almost like to have it on your gravestone. Listen:

> "For each tear you shed on earth
> my coffin fills with blood.
> But each time on earth you're truly glad
> and break leaves from tree lilies
> my coffin fills with fragrant rose.

"Isn't that nice?" said Gran.

And so that wet March Sunday rolled on toward evening.

Mia and Gran talked and sewed and slept and looked at photographs and listened to the radio and played Taube's Nocturne—twice, for Gran loved it.

Meanwhile the rain just went on pouring down and the telephone was silent. The bouquet of red roses that Gran had been given at the dinner was standing by her bed and filled the whole room with its mild scent. Mia baked an instant cardamom cake with apples for afternoon coffee, and the cardamom blended with the scent of roses into something pleasing and homey.

"What a wonderful day we've had together, the two of us," said Gran when Mia came in at about nine to help her to bed.

"I'll never forget this day," said Mia, and she bent down to kiss her grandmother.

Mia left her door ajar when she went to bed. She hadn't done that lately, but since Dad wasn't home, she felt safer that way.

In contrast to other evenings recently, she fell asleep almost at once. The wind had risen, and as she lay there dozing, she heard the gusts of rain striking the window and thought vaguely about what it had felt like the first time they had come to live on the seventh floor—like living on the upper deck of a huge Atlantic liner. It was odd that it was only a year ago since she and Lillan had sat on packing cases and sacks of bedding, staring at Datema's yellow five-pointed star, and Lillan had played at being a spaceman with a baking tin on her head. It seemed a century ago, Mia thought, and fell asleep.

She was wakened suddenly by a sound, a loud but dull sound, like something heavy falling over.

For a moment she lay still, uncertain, not knowing whether she had simply dreamed it. Then she heard a cry, and she leaped out of bed, rushed across the kitchen and into Gran's room.

The light was on. She saw Gran half on her knees by the bed. The object that had fallen over was a chair.

Gran was groaning and twisting as if she had a cramp. Mia darted over to her and tried to lift her up, but she shook her head, pressing both arms against her chest, her face chalk white and distorted with pain.

"Have you taken the nitroglycerine?" Mia said abruptly. "Gran, dear, can you hear me?"

"... I have," she whispered, "... but it didn't help ... I felt so sick ... wanted to vomit." She stopped at another stab of pain. "This ... it's not the usual ... Call the doctor ..."

"But I can't leave you like this. Isn't there anything I can do first?"

Her grandmother shook her head and groaned loudly.

Mia stumbled out into the hall, her whole body shaking as she ran her finger down the list of telephone numbers on the wall to find the doctor's. With difficulty she found the right holes to dial the number.

The calm wide-awake voice at the other end made her pull herself together.

"Oh, doctor ... Gran ... it's Mia Järeberg ... Gran's dreadfully ill, much worse than usual. What shall I do ... can you come?"

"I'll call an ambulance instead," he said quickly. "It'd be a waste of time if I try to get over to you first. It's probably a coronary. What's the address again? Twenty-nine Main Street? Will you make sure the ambulance men can get in? Your father, I presume, will come, too."

He had put down the receiver before Mia had time to answer.

She rushed back to Gran's room and saw that she had spun round and was sitting on the floor with her back to the bed. The eyes looking up at Mia were wild with agony ...

"The ambulance's coming any minute," whispered Mia comfortingly, trying to tuck a blanket around the thin little body. Oh, God, the outside door . . . how would she get it to stay open? It just closed automatically. She couldn't stay down there waiting, with Gran in such pain.

She rushed into her room, threw on some slacks and a sweater, thrust her feet into her boots, and snatched up a book to hold the door open. Without waiting for the elevator, she rushed down the emergency stairs and out onto the sidewalk . . . no ambulance . . . oh, God . . . she'd have to prop the door open.

When she got back to the apartment, she heard Gran calling her name.

"Here . . . sorry . . . I'm here . . . sorry, I had to open the outside door for the ambulance men."

Her voice broke.

"*Don't—don't leave me* . . . Mia . . . promise me." Gran panted, cold sweat pouring down her face.

"I promise . . . I'll hold your hand like this, hard. Oh, Gran, it'll soon be better, you'll see. Would you like a pillow there . . ." God in heaven, why doesn't the ambulance come. . . . Supposing there's no one on duty . . . it's Sunday night. Perhaps there've been a lot of accidents in all that rain. "Yes, Gran, it's coming soon, soon . . . I think I can hear the elevator coming up." Gran, dearest Gran, does it hurt so much? And all the whisky gone.

How long would it take to get from here to the hospital? Ten minutes . . . quarter of an hour? Perhaps she ought to call the doctor again? No, it wasn't worth leaving her.

At last the elevator stopped outside.

Two white-clad young men with calm voices came in and spoke to her.

"It's her heart . . . she must sit up," she stammered, standing helplessly to one side, watching their practiced calm hands lifting the little blue-flowered figure onto the stretcher.

"We know . . . the doctor told us what it was about."

"Her bag . . . there are her papers and that disk thing in it," said Mia, hunting blindly around the room until she found Gran's bag in its usual place, hanging on the bed-post. "Wait . . ." she snatched up her coat and ran after the stretcher. "I'll take the stairs." No, she didn't have any keys . . . her keys . . . ? She turned her bag upside down on the hall floor . . . there . . . she snatched them up and ran.

Mia was sitting on a bench outside the room in which Gran was lying.

"I want to be with her," she had cried to the doctor. "I promised I'd stay with her . . . you can't . . ."

"You can go in in a minute . . . we're just doing some tests and giving her an injection . . . she's in a lot of pain."

She had been given oxygen in the ambulance . . . things must be really bad. Mia didn't dare ask straight out.

She had had to answer a lot of questions—about how it had begun, whether Gran had overstrained herself, whether she had taken any medicine, whether she'd been sick.

"She was so well all day. We were having such a nice time . . . though she did complain she was constipated last night . . . she took some of that syrup stuff . . . her doctor had said she could go to this dinner . . . she wanted to so much."

Mia heard Gran groaning in there and she jumped to her feet. An elderly doctor was just hurrying into the room. Through the half-open door she could hear them

speaking quickly to each other, strange words . . . fibrillation
—edema.

"Oh, please can I come in? Why can't I come in?" Her
voice sounded hysterical and shrill.

"Of course, my dear, come on in." The elderly doctor
appeared in the doorway and went over to her. "But don't
be frightened—it looks a bit frightening with all the apparatus. It's a severe coronary and we can't promise . . . that
she'll make it." He took her by her shoulders and guided
her over to the bed. "Your grandmother isn't in such pain
now, but she's having difficulty breathing, as you see, so
she's being given oxygen."

Mia stood immobile by the side of the bed, watching
Gran's chest slowly slowly rising and falling. There was
something unreal about Gran's closed eyes below the
bangs . . . here in this alien bed, with all the things and
tubes and apparatus. It was as if she were a kind of object.

"May I . . . may I hold her hand?" she said.

"Of course . . . and you can try to speak to her, if you
like. But she may not be able to hear, as the injection is
beginning to work now."

Speak to her? What could you say?

Mia tried to clear her throat . . . her voice had gone.

"Gran . . . it's me, Mia. I'm here with you . . . all the
time."

She saw a spasm go through the eyelids, but the hand
lying in Mia's was mute and cold. She tried pressing it
hard, as she had done when Gran had been in pain, but
now there was no response; it just lay still, without resistance, like a dead bird.

She heard voices around her, but she didn't understand

what they were saying. She simply wondered how their faces could look so calm and unmoved.

"Is she going to die?" she whispered to no one in particular.

No one answered.

"She wasn't afraid of dying," she heard herself saying in an alien voice, as if she were someone else.

Time stood still.

Mia didn't know if ten minutes had gone past, or an hour. There was a clock on the wall, but she couldn't make out what the time was. She saw the hands standing in a certain way, then moving with a little click forward, but she could not take it in. Suddenly something had changed. Voices . . . movements.

Someone went up to the bed and bent over, uncoupling the oxygen apparatus.

"Doesn't she need it any longer?" she whispered eagerly, suddenly conscious again.

"No, my dear." The doctor came up to her and put his hand on her arm. "She doesn't need it any longer. . . . She's . . . she's dead."

Mia sat immobile as if she hadn't heard. She looked at the small white face.

"She enjoyed the party," she exclaimed, and the next moment she was weeping against someone's white chest.

The sense of unreality just went on.

You went out of a room. And you'd never see her again.

Someone was dead and people scuttled about corridors as if nothing had happened. One doctor even yawned. The nurse went to receive another patient. Gran was dead, and Mia was sitting with a kindly orderly, eating ham-and-cheese sandwiches and drinking hot chocolate out of a plastic mug.

That you could *eat*.

It should show in some way, some external way. There should be some kind of sign in the sky. The birds shouldn't sing as usual.

That you could eat and think it was good.

And then sleep like a log on a couch, waiting for the morning, waiting for the doctor to call Dad in Sigtuna to tell him that Gran was dead.

Poor Dad. It was his *mother*.

He would have an awfully guilty conscience because he hadn't been at home, perhaps thinking it wouldn't have happened if he had been.

It was seven o'clock now, and the doctor had just telephoned Dad.

Dad had asked to speak to her. He had cried and she had comforted him. "It was better for her, you see—she was in such pain."

"I'm coming back at once. Poor Mia . . . take a taxi home."

Well, yes, a taxi. That wasn't all that easy when you didn't have any money with you. Mia considered borrowing some from the nice orderly, but then decided against it. She could perfectly well walk home. She could see through the office window that it was a radiantly beautiful spring morning. I'll cut diagonally across the churchyard, then it'll be shorter, she thought.

It was a long time since she had walked around the churchyard, probably not since Lillan was a tiny baby. She and Mother had pushed the carriage along these paths when the weather was fine. She had had her doll Klara in a little carriage with a red hood.

It all felt so strange, almost like a kind of intoxication. She wasn't even tired, and if the feeling she had was sorrow, then it wasn't what she had expected.

Perhaps she would cry or have a headache or a stomach ache and so on later on. Perhaps this was a kind of shock after the horror of last night.

Her feet felt as if they wished to fly along the gravel paths. The birds were singing like mad, the scillas were already out in the lawns, like bright blue cloths scattered over the green grass.

Someone was raking leaves into a red plastic basket. The sun threw golden sparks on to the carved letters on the gravestone of P. A. Anderson, Merchant.

Mia suddenly felt so grateful, so grateful that she had liked Gran so much. It was strange, but it was easier to bear that she was dead when you liked her so much. Shouldn't it be the other way around?

It had been such a good time with Gran this spring.

But could it have gone on in the same way?

Would she have managed? And Dad and Mia?

Mia sat down on a bench.

The strong light poured down around her, the ground steaming with damp after the long spell of rain, smelling of brown earth. The buds on the bushes almost swelled as you watched them, and the birds were making a tremendous racket, drowning even the sound of the traffic on the main road on the other side of the railings.

It was strange to think that out there was a perfectly

ordinary morning for most people, with people going to work and drinking coffee and starting their cars and leafing through the paper. With kids going to school and yelling in the corridors, the stores displaying the latest spring fashions and having special offers for Saturday's chickens. Hectic young fathers rushing off to day-care centers and a police car taking two arrested men to court. It was life, the same old life as usual.

But on a bench inside the churchyard sat Mia, and for her this morning was a morning that she would remember all her life.

The morning when Gran was dead and Mia walked home along the muddy paths of the churchyard in her down-at-heel winter boots, trying to understand what grief was.

It was all so confusing.

One moment you almost danced on, filled with gratitude and love that bubbled over and was almost like joy, and the next minute a cold hand gripped your heart and you began to think that soon you would be back in the apartment.

And you would see Gran's bed and the pillows on the floor and the chair that was still overturned . . . smell the smell of medicine and eau de cologne and roses. Her cherry-red dress would still be hanging on its hanger on the closet door and her glasses would still be on the bedside table.

And then you would know what death meant—*never again*.

And Dad would come home, gray in the face, his eyes swollen, and Mother would telephone and be upset. And even if she wouldn't say it, she would think it—I've been expecting this all spring.

And everyone would be awfully kind and considerate and unnatural and it would all be very difficult.

Mia wished that she could stay sitting on this bench forever, listening to the birds and smelling the earth and thinking a little about that poem Gran had talked about . . . *Each time on earth you're truly glad . . . my coffin fills with fragrant rose.*

Perhaps she had sensed it.

And that about the man in the temple . . . Simeon.

And that *somewhere within us, we are always together*— that was good, too. Gran had thought it was outworn, but Mia had never heard it before.

You need words.

It was good when someone formulated things for you.

Mia began to feel cold. She must go home soon.

Home to that empty room and half a cardamom cake.

It was just a matter of going.

But soon those sharp memories would stop hurting, and you would just remember the good ones, the great ones, the important ones.

Perhaps one day Mia would think back to this time and say, "Oh, that was the spring when I had my eighteenth birthday . . . that fantastic spring when everything happened . . . the spring when I understood *lots* of things I hadn't understood before . . . that strange spring when the warmth came so early and everything was out for Easter.

"That spring with Gran and Dad and Martin."

ABOUT THE AUTHOR

GUNNEL BECKMAN lives in Solna, Sweden, with her husband. The mother of five children, she edited the women's
page of a daily newspaper in Gothenberg and has worked
as a probation officer. Ms. Beckman has written a number
of books for young people, two of which have been published by Viking, *A Room of His Own* and *Mia Alone*.
That Early Spring continues the story of Mia.